Dick King-Smith, a former dairy farmer, is one of the world's favourite children's book authors. He won the Guardian Fiction Award for *The Sheep-Pig* (recently filmed as *Babe*), was named Children's Book Author of the Year in 1991 and won the 1995 Children's Book Award for *Harriet's Hare*. His titles for Walker include the much-loved Sophie series (illustrated by David Parkins), *The Finger-eater* and *Dick King-Smith's Animal Friends*.

David Parkins has illustrated a number of children's books, including the picture books *No Problem*, *Prowlpuss* (shortlisted for the 1994 Kurt Maschler Award, the 1995 Smarties Book Prize and Commended in the 1995 National Art Library Awards for Illustration), *Aunt Nancy and Old Man Trouble*, *Aunt Nancy and Cousin Lazybones* and *Webster J. Duck*. His non-fiction title, *Fly Traps: Plants that Bite Back*, written by Martin Jenkins, was shortlisted for the 1997 TES Information Book Award. David lives in Lincolnshire with his family and six cats.

Books by the same author

Sophie's Further Adventures
(Sophie in the Saddle, Sophie Is Seven,
Sophie's Lucky)

The Finger-eater
Lady Lollipop

SOPHIE'S ADVENTURES

Written by
DICK KING-SMITH

Illustrated by
DAVID PARKINS

WALKER BOOKS
AND SUBSIDIARIES
LONDON · BOSTON · SYDNEY

First published individually as
Sophie's Snail (1988), *Sophie's Tom* (1991) and *Sophie Hits Six* (1991)
by Walker Books Ltd
87 Vauxhall Walk, London SE11 5HJ

This edition published 2001

2 4 6 8 10 9 7 5 3

Text © 1988, 1991 Fox Busters Ltd
Illustrations © 1991, 1994 David Parkins

The right of Dick King-Smith to be identified as author of this
work has been asserted by him in accordance with the Copyright,
Designs and Patents Act 1988

This book has been typeset in Plantin

Printed and bound in Great Britain by the Guernsey Press Co. Ltd

British Library Cataloguing in Publication Data:
a catalogue record for this book is
available from the British Library

ISBN 0-7445-7873-6

CONTENTS

SOPHIE'S
SNAIL

*Suddenly two little horns poked
up through the grating.*

CONTENTS

*"What animal has got only one foot?" said their father.
"A chicken standing on one leg!" the twins said.*

ONE VERY
SMALL FOOT

"What animal has got only one foot?" said the children's father. "I bet you can't tell me."

"I can!" said Matthew and Mark with one voice. As well as looking exactly alike, the twins nearly always said exactly the same thing at exactly the same time. Matthew was ten minutes older than Mark, but after that there had never been the slightest difference between them.

"Go on then," said their father. "Tell me. What animal's got only one foot?"

"A chicken standing on one leg!" they said.

"That's silly," said Sophie seriously.

Sophie was four, a couple of years younger than her brothers.

"That's silly," she said. "It would still have a foot on the other leg. Anyway, Daddy, there isn't really an animal that's only got one foot, is there?"

"Yes, there is, Sophie."

"What?"

"A snail. Every snail has a big flat sticky muscle under it that it travels along on. That's called its foot. Next time you see a snail crawling along, pick it up carefully and turn it over, and you'll see. There are loads in the garden."

"Come on! Let's find one!" said Matthew to Mark and Mark to Matthew at the same time.

"Wait for me," said Sophie. But they didn't, so she plodded after them.

When she caught up with the twins, in a

far corner of the garden, each was examining the underside of a large snail. Sophie was not surprised to see that the snails were also obviously twins, the same size, the same shape, the same striped greeny-browny colour.

"I know!" said Matthew.

"I know what you're going to say!" said Mark.

"Let's have a snail race!" they said.

"How are you going to tell them apart?" said Sophie.

"I know!" said Mark.

"I know what you're going to say!" said Matthew.

"Fetch us a felt pen, Sophie," they said.

"What are you going to do?" asked Sophie when she came back with a red felt pen.

"Put my initial on my snail," said Mark

"Wait for me," said Sophie.
"I haven't got a snail yet."

and Matthew together.

"But you've got the same initial."

The boys looked at each other.

"I know!" they said.

"I know what you're going to say," said Sophie, and she plodded off again. She came back with a blue felt pen.

After a moment, "Ready?" said Matthew, holding up his snail with a big red M on its shell, and at the same instant, "Ready?" said Mark, holding up his snail with a big blue M.

"Wait for me," said Sophie. "I haven't got a snail yet," but already the twins had set their twin snails side by side on the path that ran between the edge of the lawn and the flowerbed. The path was made of big oval flagstones, and they chose the largest one, perhaps a metre long. The far end of the flagstone was to be the winning post.

"Ready, steady, go!" they shouted.

Sophie plodded off. "I'll beat them," she said. She was small but very determined.

Behind the first stone she moved, almost as though it had been waiting for her, was a snail. It was as different as possible from Red M and Blue M. It was very little, no bigger than Sophie's middle fingernail, and it was a lovely buttercup yellow.

As she watched, it stretched out its head, poked out its two horns, and began to crawl, very slowly. It had a most intelligent face, Sophie thought. She picked it up carefully, and turned it over.

"What a very small-sized shoe you would take, my dear," she said. "I don't know whether you can win a race but you are very beautiful. You shall be my snail."

"Who won?" she said to Matthew and Mark when she returned.

"They didn't go the right way," they both said.

"But mine went furthest," they both said.

"No, it didn't," they both said.

They picked up their snails and put them side by side once more.

"Wait for me," Sophie said, and she put down the little yellow snail. It looked very small beside the others.

"Just look at Sophie's snail!" hooted the twins, but this time when they shouted "Ready, steady, go!" neither Red M nor Blue M would move. They stayed stubbornly inside their shells and took not the slightest notice of their owners' cries of encouragement.

Sophie's snail plodded off.

It was small but very determined, and Sophie lay on the grass beside the path and watched it putting its best foot forward.

After half an hour, it reached the winning post.

Sophie jumped up. "Mine's the winner!" she cried, but there was no one to hear. The twins had become bored with snail-racing at exactly the same time and gone away. Red M and Blue M had gone away too, into the forest of the flowerbed. Only Sophie's snail kept stoutly on, while the straight silvery trail it had left glistened in the sunshine.

Sophie knelt down and carefully put her hand flat in front of the little yellow creature. It crawled solemnly onto it.

"You have such an intelligent look, my dear," said Sophie.

"What *have* you got in your hand, Sophie?" said her mother at tea-time.

"It's Sophie's snail!" chorused Matthew and Mark.

*"You have such an intelligent look,
my dear," said Sophie.*

"Put it straight out in the garden," said the children's mother.

"No," said Sophie in a small but determined voice.

Her mother looked at her, sighed, picked up a box of matches, emptied the matches out and gave Sophie the empty box.

"Put it in there till after tea," she said, "and go and wash your hands."

All that evening Sophie played with her snail. When it was bedtime, and she was ready to wash and do her teeth, she put the snail carefully on the flat rim of the wash-basin.

Then (as she always did) she filled the basin with warm water right up to the over-flow and washed her face and hands. The snail did not move, though it appeared to be watching.

Then (as she always did) she brushed her teeth very hard, making a lot of froth in her mouth and spitting the bubbly blobs of toothpaste out on top of the rather dirty water. She always liked doing this. The toothpaste blobs made strange shapes on the surface of the water, often like a map of the world. Tonight there was a big white Africa at one side of the basin.

Then (as she always did) she pulled the plug out, but as she turned to dry her hands the sleeve of her dressing gown scuffed the rim of the basin. Right into the middle of disappearing Africa fell a small yellow shape, and then the last of the whirlpooling frothing water disappeared down the plug hole, leaving the basin quite empty.

Sophie plodded down the stairs.

"My snail's gone down the plug hole," she said in a very quiet voice.

"You couldn't have kept it, you know," said her father gently. "It would have died anyway without its natural food."

"Next time you find one," said her mother, "just leave it in the garden. There are lots of other snails there, just as nice."

"Not as nice as my snail," said Sophie. She looked so unhappy that for once the twins said different things, in an effort to comfort her.

"'Spect it died quickly," said Matthew.

"Sure to be drowned by now," said Mark.

Try as she would, Sophie could not stop herself thinking about what happened to you if you went down a plug hole. She lay in bed and thought about the twins washing their hands in the basin and washing their teeth, and then later on Mum and

Dad doing the same. All that water would be washing the body of her snail farther and farther away, down the drain into the sewer, down the sewer into the river, down the river into the sea.

When at last she slept, she dreamed that she was walking by the seaside, and there she saw, washed up on the beach, a familiar little yellow shape. But when she ran and picked it up, it had no head, no horns, no foot. It was just an empty snail shell.

Sophie woke early with the feeling that something awful had happened, and then she remembered what it was.

She plodded along to the bathroom and looked over the rim of the washbasin at the round plug hole with its metal grating meant to stop things going down it.

"But you were too small," she said.

Leaning over as far as she could reach,

"Goodbye, my dear," said Sophie.
"I hope we meet again."

she stared sadly into the black depths of the plug hole. And as she stared, suddenly two little horns poked up through the grating, and then a head, and then a shell no bigger than her middle fingernail, a shell that was a lovely buttercup yellow.

Very carefully Sophie reached out and picked up her small determined snail.

Very quietly she plodded down the stairs and opened the back door and went out into the garden and crossed the dewy lawn.

Very gently, at the exact spot she had found it, she put her snail down and watched it slowly move away on its very small foot.

"Goodbye, my dear," said Sophie. "I hope we meet again," and then she sat happily on the wet grass watching, till at last there was nothing more to be seen of Sophie's snail.

*Next morning, Sophie came in to
breakfast carrying her piggy bank.*

FARM
MUNNY

"When I grow up," said Sophie at breakfast time, "I'm going to be a farmer."

"You can't," said the twins.

"Why not?"

"Farmers are men," they said.

"Well," said Sophie, "I'm going to be a lady farmer. So there."

Her father looked at her over the top of his newspaper.

"I'm sure you are, Sophie," he said. "I'm sure you could do anything you were determined to do. But you'd need an awful lot of money. Suppose you wanted to be a dairy farmer. Just think how much a big herd of cows would cost."

"I wouldn't have a big herd of cows," said Sophie.

"How many would you have?" asked Mark.

"I'd just have one cow, called Blossom."

"Well then, you wouldn't have much milk to sell," said her father.

"I wouldn't have any milk to sell," said Sophie.

"Why not?" asked Matthew.

"I should drink it all. I like milk."

She held out her glass.

"Can I have some more please, Mum?" she said.

"I don't really think," said her mother, "that you could call yourself a farmer..."

"A lady farmer," said the twins.

"...if the only thing you had was one cow."

"It wouldn't be the only thing," Sophie

said. "I'd have two hens, called April and May."

"Why April?" said Matthew.

"Why May?" said Mark.

"Because they're nice months. And these would be nice hens."

"You wouldn't have many eggs to sell," said her father.

"I wouldn't have any eggs to sell," said Sophie.

"Because you'd eat them all," said Mark.

"Because you like eggs," said Matthew.

"I do," said Sophie. "I'm very fond of eggs."

She looked at the boiled egg which her mother had just put in front of her. Sophie had her own special blue egg cup with her name written on it in white letters. The egg was a big brown one.

"Excuse me, my dear," said Sophie, and

*Sophie tapped the egg gently with her spoon.
"I don't think it hurts them," she said.*

she tapped it gently with her spoon. "I don't think it hurts them," she said.

Matthew and Mark looked at each other, and each rolled his eyes upwards and raised his eyebrows and tapped his forehead with one finger.

"What other animals will you keep?" said Sophie's father.

"A pony."

"What kind of pony?"

"A Shetland pony. I like Shetland ponies."

"But Sophie," said her mother, "don't you think a Shetland pony will be rather small for you when you're a grown-up lady farmer? I mean, your legs will drag along the ground."

"I shan't ride it," said Sophie. "It'll just be a pet. I shall call it Shorty."

"What other pets will you keep?"

"Just a pig."

"Pigs aren't pets," said the twins.

"Measles will be."

"Why Measles?"

"Because he'll be a spotty pig, of course," said Sophie, looking scornfully at her brothers. "You've got no imagination, you two haven't."

She scraped the last bits out of her boiled egg and then turned it upside down on top of the egg cup so that it looked untouched.

"There you are, my dear," she said. "Good as new."

"Let me see if I've got it right," said her father. "When you're a lady farmer, you're going to keep a cow and two hens and a pony and a pig. Am I right?"

"Yes," said Sophie. "And I shall grow a little field of corn."

"What for?" said Matthew and Mark.

*"Measles will be a
spotty pig," said Sophie.*

"Cornflakes, of course," said Sophie. "Don't they teach you anything at school?"

"But what are you going to live on?" asked her father.

"Milk and eggs and cornflakes. I'm very fond of all those."

"No, no, I mean how are you going to manage? None of the animals – Blossom and April and May and Shorty and Measles – is going to earn you any money. And how will you afford to buy them in the first place?"

"I shall save up."

"But that will take you years and years and years," said the twins.

"I've got years and years and years," said Sophie. With that she got down from the table and plodded off.

"She'll never get enough money to be a lady farmer," said Matthew.

"Will she, Dad?" asked Mark.

"I wouldn't be too sure about that," said their father. "Your sister may be small but she is a very determined person."

So nobody was very surprised next morning when Sophie came in to breakfast carrying her piggy bank and placed it on the table.

On its side was stuck a notice, which said:

FARM MUNNY

THANK YOU

SOPHIE

Sophie's father put his hand in his pocket and took out a 20p piece and dropped it in. Her mother fetched her bag and added another.

Matthew and Mark looked at each other.

"I've only got 2p," said Matthew.

"Same here," said Mark.

"Every little helps," said Sophie.

"Yikes!" said Sophie.
"She must be enormous!"

AUNT
ALICE

The children's father looked up from the letter he was reading.

"It's from Aunt Alice," he said in rather a surprised voice. "She's coming to see us."

"Who's Aunt Alice?" asked the twins.

"She's Daddy's aunt," said their mother. "Or rather she's Grandpa's aunt, so she's Daddy's great-aunt."

"I've never seen a great aunt," Sophie said.

"Well, of course, she's more than that to you three children. She's a great-great-aunt."

"Yikes!" said Sophie. "She must be *enormous!*"

"You'll soon be able to see," said her father. "She's asked herself to lunch next Sunday."

"Why haven't we seen her before?" asked Matthew and Mark.

"Because she lives about six hundred miles away, in the Highlands of Scotland."

"It's a long way to come for lunch," said Sophie.

"No, no, she's already down this way, staying in London for a few days."

The twins forgot almost at once about the coming visit of Great-great-aunt Alice, but Sophie didn't.

She wondered about the Highlands. How did you get down from them? On a rope? Or a ladder?

She wondered about this great-great-aunt. How would she get to London? In a train? But she might be too big to get through the carriage door. In an aeroplane perhaps? Yes, that would be best, in one of those huge ones with fat tummies that you could put tanks and lorries and things inside. The plane could fly off the top of the Highlands and then, when it got to London, they could open the big doors at the back and this enormous aunt could walk out.

But when Sunday came, and the front door opened, it was a very small person who walked in. The top of her head, Sophie could see, didn't even come up to Daddy's shoulder.

"Now then, Aunt Al," Sophie's father said, "these are the twins, Matthew and Mark."

"How de do?" said Aunt Alice, and she shook each boy's hand in turn.

Although it wasn't always so, Matthew and Mark happened this day to be wearing

"I'm four," said Sophie.
"How old are you?"

exactly the same clothes.

"Like as two peas in a pod," said Aunt Alice. "Which is which?"

"I'm Matthew," said Matthew.

"I'm Mark," said Mark.

"I'm nearly ten minutes older," said Matthew.

"And I'm two years younger," said Sophie.

"Ah!" said Aunt Alice. "Now you must be Sophie." She took hold of Sophie's hand and held it, looking at her with sharp blue eyes. She looked rather like a bird, Sophie thought, with those bright eyes and a thin beaky nose and hands that were skinny and bony and curled like a bird's claws.

"And how old are you, Sophie?" she said.

"I'm four," said Sophie. "How old are you?"

"Sophie!" said her mother. "You can't go

asking things like that!"

"Why not?" said Sophie. "She asked me, didn't you?"

"Quite right," said Aunt Alice. "Load of rubbish, people not wanting to tell their age. I'm eighty. And I'm hungry as a hunter. When's lunch?"

After lunch, Sophie and Aunt Alice sat on a swing-seat on the lawn. Sophie's parents were doing the washing-up and the twins were playing with a football at the far end of the garden.

Aunt Alice's small shoes just touched the ground, and she swung the seat gently back and forth. Sophie sat beside her, feet sticking straight out, and looked directly at the bird-face. I don't know about a great-great-aunt, she thought. Looks to me more like a small-small-aunt.

"What shall I call you?" she said.

"Same as everyone else does. Aunt Al. It's nice and short, like me."

"Are the Highlands very high, Aunt Al?" said Sophie.

"Quite high."

"And cold?"

"Quite cold."

"Lots of snow?"

"Masses, in winter."

"Polar bears?"

"No," said Aunt Alice. "But lots of lovely creatures, like golden eagles and blue hares and red deer."

They swung in silence for a while

Then Sophie said, "It sounds nice. I wouldn't have bothered coming down off the top of the Highlands to go to London if I were you."

"I don't often. But there were a few

things that I wanted to do."

"Like coming to lunch with us?"

"Of course. And doing some shopping. And seeing about my will."

"What's the matter with your Will?" said Sophie. "Is he ill?"

Aunt Alice gave a little chirp of amusement, but before she could answer, the twins came running up and stood side by side in front of her, grinning.

Sophie sighed.

She knew those identical grins.

She knew what was coming.

Still sighing, she wriggled down from the swing-seat and plodded off.

Aunt Alice looked at the two boys.

"Hello," she said.

"Hello," they said.

"Guess . . . " said Matthew.

" . . . which is which," said Mark.

*Sophie wriggled down from
the swing-seat and plodded off.*

"Bet you can't tell," they said.

It was a game they never tired of playing. If the visitor guessed wrong anyway, well and good. But if the guess was right, if the visitor pointed at Matthew and said "You're Matthew," he would reply "Mark"; and if Mark was correctly chosen, he would answer "Matthew". So they always won.

Sophie did not approve of this.

"You tell lies," she said severely.

"No, we don't," they said. "We just say each other's name. That's not telling lies."

However, Sophie did not approve of telling tales either, so she had never said anything. Still, she would not watch when they played this game on people, but always stumped off.

Aunt Alice looked at the grinning twins.

"Bet I can," she said.

She opened her bag and took out her

purse. From it she took two pound coins.

"Tell you what," she said. "If I'm wrong, you each get one of these."

"All right!" they cried eagerly.

Aunt Alice stared long and carefully at each boy in turn, nodding her neat head up and down as if she were a thrush choosing between two worms. Then suddenly, like a bird pecking, she said, "Quick! Which of you's the older?" Before he could stop himself, Matthew twitched his mouth.

Aunt Alice looked at him poker-faced.

"You," she said deliberately, "are . . . Mark."

"No!" they both shouted delightedly. "No! You're wrong!"

"Honestly?" said Aunt Alice.

"Honestly," they said.

"In that case, I'd better pay up."

*   *   *

When Matthew and Mark had run off whooping and cheering, Sophie came plodding back. She climbed on to the swingseat.

"I've just been guessing which twin was which," Aunt Alice said.

"Huh!" said Sophie. She sighed.

"What ever can you mean?" said Aunt Alice.

Sophie looked very directly at her great-great-aunt.

"Aunt Al," she said. "Can you keep a secret?"

"Sure thing."

"Sometimes one of them pretends to be the other."

"Disgraceful," said Aunt Alice. "What wicked boys."

"I don't know," said Sophie. "They're all right really. They just get overexcited."

"Aunt Al," Sophie said.
"Can you keep a secret?"

They sat side by side, swinging gently. For some time neither spoke. Each was comfortable with the silence.

Then Sophie said, "Did you give them money?"

"Yes."

"They'll only spend it."

"Wouldn't you, if I gave you money?"

"No, I'd save it. I'm saving up for a farm."

"A toy one?"

"No, a real one."

"Whew! That'll take a long time."

"I expect it will," said Sophie.

Aunt Alice looked very directly at her great-great-niece.

"Sophie," she said. "Can you keep a secret?"

"Sure thing."

Aunt Alice took out her purse again.

"I gave the boys a pound each," she said, "but I'm going to give you two," and she did.

"Yikes!" said Sophie. "Thanks!"

"After all," said Aunt Alice with a grin, "it's not your fault that you're not twins."

When the twins found Sophie and asked her to play football, she said she was too busy.

DAWN

"What shall we do this morning, Matthew?" said Mark.

"I know!" said Matthew.

"I know what you're going to say!" said Mark.

"Let's go and play football!" they said.

"Mum!" they shouted. "We're going out to play football."

"Well, take Sophie with you."

"She doesn't much like football."

"You never ask her. Go and ask her now." But when they found Sophie and asked her, she said she was too busy. So they went without her.

A little later Sophie's mother went out into

the garden and found Sophie plodding round, peering into the flowerbeds as though searching for something. She was carrying a small yellow bucket.

"Why didn't you go with the twins?" her mother said.

"Too busy," grunted Sophie.

She bent down and picked up a spent matchstick and put it in her bucket.

"Oh, you are a good girl, Sophie," said her mother, "picking up Daddy's old matchsticks. Every time he smokes his pipe he uses dozens of matches to keep the wretched thing alight, and then he chucks the used ones all over the garden. But wouldn't you rather be playing with the others than just picking up matchsticks?"

"I'm not just picking up matchsticks," said Sophie severely. "I'm collecting food for all of my animals."

Sophie's mother went back to her housework shaking her head. She's getting to be a proper loner, she thought. Collecting food for her animals indeed! Whoever heard of animals eating wood! She lives in a world of her own. It's not good for her. I wish there was a girl of her own age for her to play with.

A couple of weeks later, Sophie's mother's wish was granted. A nearby house changed hands and the new people who moved in had a little girl who looked to be just about Sophie's age, a pretty little girl with golden hair done in bunches.

Sophie's mother lost no time in making contact.

"Sophie," she said one morning. "Those new people down the road have got a little girl."

"I know," said Sophie. "I've seen her. She wears frocks."

Sophie did not approve of frocks.

"She's called Dawn," said her mother.

"Yuk," said Sophie. She thrust her hands into the pockets of her old jeans and stumped off, shoulders hunched, the very picture of disapproval.

"I've asked them round this morning," her mother called after her. She turned to the twins. "You three children can play with Dawn while we're having coffee," she said.

"What time are they coming?" said Matthew.

"Eleven o'clock."

"We've got a football match," said Mark.

"Kick-off half past ten sharp," they said.

* * *

Sophie stumped off, shoulders hunched,
the very picture of disapproval.

Dawn held out her toy pony.
"This is Twinkletoes," she said.

Dawn was wearing a green dress with bows on it, and long white socks, and smart red shoes. Her bunches were tied with green ribbon. She carried a little toy pony.

Dawn's mother raised her eyebrows just a tiny bit as Sophie was called up to be introduced.

Sophie was wearing an old blue jersey with her name written on it in white letters, and her old jeans, and her muddy wellies. Her dark hair looked as though she had just come through a hedge backwards. She carried her yellow bucket.

"Sophie," said her mother. "This is Dawn."

Dawn held out her toy pony. It was a bright pink pony with a long silvery mane and tail. It even had long silvery nylon eyelashes.

"This is Twinkletoes," she said. "He's

my special favourite. But you can play with him if you like."

Sophie stared woodenly at Twinkletoes. It was plain from her expression that she did not approve of pink ponies.

"Yes, off you go and play," said Sophie's mother. "And, Sophie, you look after Dawn, there's a good girl."

Sophie stumped off with Dawn prancing beside her crying, "Gee-up, Twinkletoes! Gee-up, little pony!"

They came to the nearest flowerbed, and Sophie began to hunt about.

"What are you looking for, Sophie?" asked Dawn.

"Matchsticks," said Sophie shortly. She found a couple and put them in her bucket.

"Ugh!" said Dawn, wrinkling her nose. "Nasty old matchsticks! Whatever d'you want them for?"

"To feed my animals on," said Sophie.

Dawn laughed. "You are silly, Sophie," she said. "Matchsticks are made of wood. Animals don't eat wood."

"Mine do," said Sophie.

"Isn't she silly, Twinkletoes?" said Dawn to her pony. "You wouldn't eat dirty old matchsticks, would you? You like nice grass," and she pulled some from the lawn and held them against the pink muzzle.

"You're just pretending to feed it," said Sophie scornfully. "My animals are real. I'll show you."

At the bottom of the garden was an old potting-shed. Outside it, because they were too large to fit on the shelves, stood several very big flowerpots, upside down.

Carefully Sophie tipped one of the big pots over. Underneath it, on a bed of spent matchsticks, was a great army of woodlice.

"Good morning, my dears," said Sophie. "Here's two more nice juicy matchsticks for you."

"Ugh!" said Dawn, clasping Twinkle-toes closely to her. "Horrible dirty creepy-crawlies!"

At that moment a large woodlouse de-tached itself from the mass and began to walk towards her feet.

Very deliberately, Dawn placed one of her smart red shoes on it and squashed it flat.

The yells from the bottom of the garden brought both mothers running. A dramatic scene met their eyes.

In front of the potting-shed a small, stocky figure was jumping solemnly, up and down, wellies together, on what had once been a bright pink pony with a silvery mane

*Sophie was jumping solemnly up and down
on what had once been a bright pink pony.*

and tail but was now a dirty squashed lump.

"Sophie!" cried Sophie's mother.

"Dawn, darling!" cried Dawn's mother.

"Waaaaaaa!" cried Dawn.

Sophie gave one final stamp on the battered body of Twinkletoes, and plodded off.

"Where's Sophie?" asked the twins when they came back from their game.

"She's in her room. She's been extremely naughty."

"What did she do?"

"Never you mind."

"Where's Sophie?" asked her father when he came back from work.

"She's in her room. She's been extremely naughty."

"What did she do?"

"She completely ruined a toy belonging to the child of those new people down the road. Jumped on it. Squashed it."

"Why did she do that?"

"I don't know. I've asked her, but she won't answer."

"She'll answer me," Sophie's father said. A few minutes later he came back.

"She won't," he said.

Even before Dawn's mother had said a frosty goodbye and taken her yelling daughter away, Sophie had gone straight to her room. She judged it better to go to her room than to be sent there. She sat on the side of her bed, thinking sadly of the death of the woodlouse. After a while the sad thoughts became glad ones. Dawn had paid for that! She would have to pay too, out of her Farm Money, but it would be worth it!

At bedtime the twins looked in on Sophie. They sat on the end of her bed, Matthew on one side and Mark on the other.

"What did you do?" they said.

"I busted Dawn's toy," said Sophie. "I jumped on it."

"Why?" said Mark.

"She squashed one of my woodlouses," said Sophie.

"Squashed it dead?" said Matthew.

"Yes."

"What a beastly girl," they said.

"And the toy was a horrible pink pony called Twinkletoes."

"Yuk!" they said.

"You were right to jump on it," said Matthew.

"You should have jumped on her too," said Mark.

"Did you tell Mum and Dad what she did?" they asked.

"No," said Sophie. "They'd only say 'I'm

sure she didn't mean to' or 'It was only a woodlouse after all.'"

A little later Sophie's mother and father came in. They sat on the end of Sophie's bed, one on each side.

"You know, Sophie," said her father, "you simply can't go breaking other children's toys."

"I can," said Sophie. "I just have."

"You'll have to say you're sorry," said her mother.

"I can't," said Sophie. "I'm not."

"Look, Sophie," they said, "we know what Dawn did. The boys told us." Sophie waited.

"I'm sure she didn't mean to," said her mother.

"It was only a woodlouse," said her father, "after all."

Sophie was walking round the garden,
wearing a pair of her mother's sunglasses.

A BAD
BACK

Sophie was walking round the garden, wearing a pair of her mother's sunglasses. They were very dark glasses with a white frame. They made Sophie look like a panda. They made pink flowers look red and yellow flowers look golden and cabbages look blue.

Sophie walked along the path that ran along the front of the house and peered in through the dining-room window. Inside, everything looked very dark, the dining table, the chairs, the dresser with its rows of plates. The wood-block floor, usually the colour of milk chocolate, had turned to plain. But whatever in the world was that long shadowy thing lying on the floor?

"Yikes!" shouted Sophie. "It's a dead body!" and she galloped off down the path and through the back door and into the kitchen.

"Mum!" she cried. "There's a dead body on the dining-room floor."

" A dead body?" said her mother, busy stirring something. "I hope not, Sophie. But you're right. There is a body on the dining-room floor."

"Whose?" said Sophie in a strangled voice.

Her mother turned from the cooker.

"Goodness me!" she said. "You look like a panda. Take those things off. No wonder you couldn't recognize your own father."

In the dining room Sophie's father lay flat on the hard wood-block floor, his arms by his sides, and stared gloomily at the ceiling.

Sophie peeped round the door.

"Daddy?" she said.

"Yes."

"Are you all right?"

"No."

"What's the matter?"

"My back hurts."

"I'm not surprised," said Sophie. "Lying on that hard old floor. If you wanted to have a rest, why didn't you go to bed?"

Sophie's father sighed.

"It's not because I'm lying on the floor that my back hurts," he said. "It's because my back hurts that I'm lying on the floor."

"Oh," said Sophie. She walked across the room and stood, feet apart, hands on hips, staring down at her father's upturned face with a worried frown on her own. "What have you done to your back?" she said.

71

*"What have you done to
your back?"* asked Sophie.

"I don't know," said her father in a grumpy voice. "All I did was bend down to pick up a newspaper and something went *click*."

"And it hurt?"

"It certainly did."

"Does it now?"

"It's OK as long as I keep still and flat like this. It's the best thing to do, they say, but it's pretty boring."

Sophie lay down beside her father, her arms by her sides, and stared thoughtfully at the ceiling.

"Would you like to play a game?" she said.

"Not if there's any moving about in it."

"No," said Sophie. "We can play I Spy. You'll only need to move your eyes. That won't hurt your back. Playing I Spy will take your mind off it."

"Oh, all right," said her father. "You start."

"I spy," said Sophie, "with my little eye, something beginning with ... s."

Sophie's father swivelled his eyes around the room. There was a row of saucers on the dresser.

"Saucer," he said.

"No."

He looked at the hanging light.

"Shade," he said.

"No."

On the wall there were pictures.

"Seaside," he said.

"You mustn't cheat, Daddy," said Sophie severely. "You can't see the seaside. It's miles and miles away."

"Yes, I can, in that picture."

"Oh. No, it's not that."

"I give up."

"You can't," said Sophie. "You can't just give up. But I'll give you a hint if you like."

"Go on then."

"Look above your head."

Sophie's father stared upwards.

"All I can see is the ceiling," he said.

"I knew you'd get it," said Sophie, "if you kept trying."

"Actually, Sophie," said her father, "*ceiling* begins with a *c*."

"How silly of it," said Sophie. "Well, then it doesn't count. It's my turn again."

Half an hour later Sophie's mother came in.

"Oh, I see you're being looked after," she said. "Perhaps you'll be a nurse when you grow up, Sophie."

"You know I'm going to be a lady farmer. Go on, Daddy, it's your turn."

"What are you playing?" said her mother.

"We're playing I Spy," said Sophie. "I'm winning."

"I think you've won," said her father hollowly. "We've spied every single thing in the room. Why don't you run out in the garden now?"

"Oh no," said Sophie. "It's much more fun playing with you. I know lots more games. I'll just go and get some things," and she plodded off.

Sophie's mother smiled.

"Poor old chap," she said. "You're a prisoner. You can't escape."

"I don't know how much more play I can stand," said Sophie's father.

"You'll just have to take it all lying down," said Sophie's mother. "The longer you can stay there, the better," and she went out just as Sophie returned with her arms full. She was carrying paper and

Sophie returned
with her arms full.

pencils, a draughts board and a box of draughts, a pack of cards and a set of Happy Families.

"There!" said Sophie, dumping them all beside her father. "That'll do for a start."

"I can't play all those games," said her father desperately. "Not when I'm lying flat."

"You can hold things in your hands, can't you?" said Sophie.

"I suppose so."

"Right. Here's a pencil and paper then. We'll begin with Noughts and Crosses."

At the end of a long, long morning, Sophie's mother came in again.

Sophie was sitting cross-legged beside her father. On her face was a look of triumph.

"Please can I have Miss Bun the Baker's Daughter?" she said. "And Master Bones the Butcher's Son?"

She pointed at the one remaining card.

"You," she said, "must be Doctor Dose the Doctor."

Wearily her father handed over Doctor Dose. His face wore a look of great suffering.

"Is it your back?" Sophie's mother said. "Is it worse?"

Sophie's father moved his head from side to side on the floor.

"No," he said. "I haven't had time to think about it."

"We've had loads of games," Sophie said. "I won nearly all of them."

"Go and wash your hands for lunch, Sophie," her mother said and, when Sophie had gone out, "How are you going to manage? Can you eat down there? The doctor should be here soon. Hadn't you better stay there till he comes?"

"Hullo," Sophie said.
"Is your name Dose?"

"I . . . am . . . not . . . staying . . . one . . . minute . . . longer," said Sophie's father.

Very carefully, he levered himself to his feet.

Very gingerly, he took a couple of steps towards the door.

"It does feel better," he said in a tone of surprise.

"I told you so, Daddy," said Sophie, coming back. "I told you playing games would take your mind off it."

In the middle of lunch the doorbell rang. Sophie answered it. It was the doctor.

"Hello," she said. "Is your name Dose?"

"Dose?" said the doctor. "No, it's Macdonald.'

"Oh," said Sophie. "Well, come in anyway."

"What's this I hear?" said the doctor,

81

*"There's only one way to deal
with a bad back," said the doctor.*

coming into the dining room. "Trouble in this happy family? Done your back in, have you?"

"It feels a lot better now," said Sophie's father.

"Does it?" said the doctor. "Well, I can tell you one thing for sure, before I even have a look at you. There's only one way to deal with a bad back."

"There is?" said Sophie's father.

"Yes. The moment you've finished lunch, you lie down flat on it, on this nice hard wooden floor, and you stay there the rest of the day."

He turned to Sophie.

"You'll keep Daddy company, won't you?" he said. "Perhaps you could think of some games to play."

One of the Bad Things about Going to School would be having to wear School Uniform.

SUCH AN
INTELLIGENT
LOOK

It was September and the twins had just gone back to school. Next term Sophie would be going too. She thought about this and wondered if she would like it. There would be Good Things and Bad Things about Going to School.

The Bad Things would be:

1. Having to wear School Uniform.
2. Having to meet Dawn again, for Dawn was starting this very term.
3. Having to meet other Strange Children, as awful as Dawn.
4. Having to meet strange Grown-ups; the Teachers might be awful too; Matthew and Mark said that they weren't, but

Sophie fancied throwing
someone down – Dawn perhaps.

you could never tell.

5. Having to eat School Lunches, especially pilchards in tomato sauce.

Of course there would be Good Things too, thought Sophie.

1. Not having to help wash up the breakfast things at home.

2. Being with her brothers in term time: She did not know that once she was at school they would not take the slightest notice of her.

3. Drinking Morning Milk: At home Mum always said, "If you're thirsty, have a drink of water – milk's fattening," but Sophie knew at school you were encouraged to drink your Morning Milk and sometimes there were extra bottles if children were away.

4. Doing Judo: Sophie fancied throwing someone down – Dawn perhaps.

5. Farming Lessons: You went to school, Sophie knew, to be taught things, for when you were grown-up. They would say, "What are you going to be?" and she'd say, "A lady farmer," and then they'd give her Farming Lessons.

Sophie's present farming was carried out in the potting-shed. Here she kept her flocks and herds.

She had a new system of free-range wood-louse farming. She had given up collecting matchsticks, which they didn't much seem to like, and now kept the woodlice in a seed tray so that they could come and go as they pleased, and fed them on cornflakes; the cornflakes seemed to disappear though she had never actually seen a woodlouse chewing one.

This morning there were only three wood-lice in the seed tray, and one of those was lying upside down, its seven pairs of legs pointed at the roof of the potting-shed.

"I hope *you* haven't hurt your back, my dear," said Sophie, grinning, as she tipped it the right way up. She dropped a couple of cornflakes into the tray.

"I wonder where the rest of the herd has got to?" she said.

On a country holiday Sophie had once seen a farmer calling in his dairy herd for milking. "Cow! Cow! Cow!" he had shouted, and the big black-and-white animals had all started walking across the field towards him.

"Louse! Louse! Louse!" Sophie shouted, but nobody came so she ate the rest of the handful of cornflakes. She went on to inspect the rest of her stock, in their various pens on a old table in the shed.

First there was a shoe box. On it was

"These shouldn't upset you, my dears,"
said Sophie. "They're digestives."

written SENTIPEEDS. There were two in it, one large and dark, one small and ginger. Sophie was planning to increase the size of this flock, but wild centipedes were difficult animals to capture, so quickly did they scuttle. She was not sure what they ate and was trying them with biscuit crumbs.

"These shouldn't upset you, my dears," she said. "They're digestives."

Next, there was an old cake tin full of soil and earthworms. Earthworms ate earth, Sophie knew, so there were no feeding problems here. She was only really interested in the largest worms, and measured her captures with an old wooden ruler. This was difficult, because it takes two people to stretch out a wriggling worm and she needed Matthew or Mark to hold one end. Her record to date was a giant of fifteen centimetres.

Beyond the worm tin was another shoe box marked YEAR WIGS. Earwig-keeping was a branch of Sophie's farming that she had only recently taken up, thanks to her great-great-aunt. Before Aunt Al's visit, Sophie had been wary of these dangerous-looking beasts with their crescent-shaped nippers.

"They bite," she had said.

"Load of rubbish," Aunt Al had said. "No good being scared of animals if you're going to be a farmer. Go and catch one and bring it here." And Sophie had caught one (cautiously, using an empty matchbox as a trap), and Aunt Al had picked it out and it hadn't bitten her.

"You have to be firm with them," she had said. "Don't stand any nonsense."

So now Sophie collected earwigs (still using the matchbox), and fed them on fruit.

She dropped a rotten plum into the box before moving on to a coffee jar, on whose glass wall hung a single enormous slug. It was dark brown in colour, with a lovely orange rim around its huge sticky foot. Sophie put a bit of cabbage leaf into the jar. She was quite proud of this monster, whose capture had covered her hands in a thick slime that took pumice stone to get off.

But her favourite animals were in the last pen of all, a large cardboard box, and she opened the lid of this and tore up the rest of the cabbage leaf and dropped it in. Under the black printed lettering on the side of the box (which said BAKED BEANS) was a single word in big red capital letters (which said SNALES).

Ever since the day of the Great Snail Race, Sophie had become especially fond of these creatures. She would spend ages watching them crawl along in their dignified way, wiggling their stalky eyes and leaving glistening silvery trails on the potting-shed table.

Every day Sophie would go on a snail hunt around the garden, adding to her herd, and there were seldom less than twenty in the box, of all shapes and sizes and shades of green or brown. The number varied, because Sophie had cut a lot of snail-sized holes in the lid of the large box, so that any-one who wished could leave.

But always in the back of Sophie's mind – as she turned over stones or peered into cracks in the garden wall or searched in the flowerbeds – was the hope that one day, perhaps she just might meet again one very particular snail.

"What did you have for lunch?" Sophie

*Every day Sophie would go on a snail hunt
around the garden, adding to her herd.*

asked the twins when they came home from school.

"Pilchards in tomato sauce," they said.

Sophie's face fell.

"Did you see Dawn?" she said.

"Yes," said Matthew. "She's got a new pony."

"A blue one," said Mark.

"Were there lots of Strange Children?"

"Lots."

"Very strange."

Sophie tried a couple of Good Things.

"Did you do Judo?" she said.

"Only juniors do Judo," they said.

"Well, did you have Farming Lessons?"

Matthew and Mark looked at each other, and each rolled his eyes upwards and raised his eyebrows and tapped his forehead with one finger.

Gloomily, Sophie stumped off.

But after that, the day improved.

First, she found a large earwig and actually caught it with her bare hands. Then she found a very pretty caterpillar which she put into a small box in the potting-shed. She was not too sure how to spell it, so she simply wrote CAT on the box.

Good luck comes in threes, thought Sophie that evening as she gazed out of her bedroom window. It was a beautiful September evening. No one could possibly have been unhappy on such an evening, not even faced with pilchards in tomato sauce.

Sophie leaned on the sill and played with a little tendril that was trying to creep across it unnoticed. She looked straight down the creeper-covered wall and there, right under her nose and climbing up towards it, was a very small snail, a snail no bigger than Sophie's middle fingernail, a

"Good evening, my dear," Sophie said softly.
"What took you so long?"

snail that was a lovely buttercup yellow.

Very slowly (but very determinedly) it plodded up the last few inches of wall and over the edge of the windowsill. Then it stopped and raised its head in greeting. It had such an intelligent look.

Sophie's face lit up in one enormous grin.

"Good evening, my dear," she said softly. "What took you so long?"

SOPHIE'S TOM

Sophie, though small,
was very determined.

CONTENTS

*Sophie woke early on the morning
of her fifth birthday.*

IN WHICH TOM APPEARS

Sophie woke early on the morning of her fifth birthday. It was still very dark. Usually the first thing she did when she had switched on the light was to look at the pictures hanging on her bedroom walls. There were four of them, all drawn by Sophie's mother who was clever at that sort of thing.

One was of a cow called Blossom, one was of two hens named April and May, the third of a Shetland pony called Shorty and the fourth of a spotty pig by the name of Measles.

These were the animals that would one day in the future belong to Sophie, for she was, she said, going to be a lady farmer when she grew up; and neither Sophie's mother and father nor her seven-year-old twin brothers, Matthew and Mark, doubted for one moment that she would.

Sophie, though small, was very determined.

But on this particular morning Sophie did not spare a glance for her portrait gallery. Instead she scrambled to the end of her bed and peered over. And there it was!

"Yikes!" cried Sophie. "He's been!" and she undid the safety-pin that fastened the long bulging woollen stocking to the bedclothes.

By now Sophie was used to the fact that her birthday was on Christmas Day. The twins, who had been born in spring, felt rather sorry for her.

"Poor old Sophie," said Matthew, "being born then."

"Hard luck on her," said Mark. "Glad we weren't."

But Sophie didn't mind.

"It's twice as nice," she said, when anyone asked how she felt about it. "Everybody gives me two presents."

"It was clever of you, Mum," she had said to her mother once.

"What was?"

"Having me on Christmas Day. How did you manage it?"

"With difficulty. But you were the nicest possible Christmas present. Daddy and I both wanted a little girl very much."

"Why?"

"Well, we already had two boys, didn't we?"

"What would you have called me if I'd been a boy?"

"Noël, probably."

"Yuk!" said Sophie. "I'm glad I wasn't, then."

This Christmas Day, the sixth of Sophie's life, started off in the customary way. As soon as the grandmother clock in the hall had struck seven, the twins ran, and Sophie plodded, into their parents' bedroom, and they all climbed on to the big bed to show what Father Christmas had brought them.

Then, after breakfast, came the ceremony of the present-giving.

This was always done in the same way. Everybody sat down, in the sitting-room of course – at least the two grown-ups sat down with their cups of coffee, while Matthew and Mark danced about with

Matthew and Mark danced about, and Sophie
stood stolidly beside the Christmas tree.

excitement, and their sister stood stolidly beside the Christmas tree, beneath which all the presents were arranged, and waited for the others to sing "Happy birthday, dear Sophie, happy birthday to you!"

Then the opening of the presents began, one at a time, youngest first, eldest last – a Christmas present for Sophie, then one for Mark, then Matthew (ten minutes older), then Mummy, then Dad, and finally a birthday present for Sophie, before she began again on her next Christmas one.

This year, to Sophie's surprise and delight, word of her intention to be a lady farmer had somehow got round the entire family, and both her Christmas and her birthday presents reflected this.

From grandparents and aunts and uncles came picture books of farms and story books of farms and colouring books of farms. Best of all, from her mother and father, there was (for Christmas) a model farmyard with a cowshed and a barn and some post-and-rail fences and a duck pond made of a piece of glass in one corner and (for her birthday) lots of little model animals, cows and sheep and horses, some standing up, some lying down, and a fierce-looking bull, chickens, a turkey-cock, some ducks for the pond, and even a spotty pig.

And as for her present from the twins – that was super, nothing less than a red tractor pulling a yellow trailer!

"The tractor's for your birthday," said Matthew.

"And the trailer's for Christmas," said Mark.

"What a lovely present!" said Sophie's mother.

"Yes," said the twins with one voice.
"It was jolly expensive too."

"Yes," said the twins with one voice. "It was jolly expensive too."

Sophie felt a bit guilty about this, since her Christmas present to them was the usual one – a Mars bar each, their favourite. Still, that was all she could manage when she had finished buying presents for her parents. Afterwards she had unscrewed the plug in the tummy of her piggy-bank, on whose side was stuck a notice:

FARM MUNNY
THANK YOU
SOPHIE

and found that there was only seven pence of her savings left.

At last there was only one present remaining at the foot of the tree, an ordinary white envelope with SOPHIE written on it.

Underneath there was some joined-up writing that Sophie couldn't read. She had left it till last because it looked boring. Probably just an old Christmas card, she thought, as she picked it up and handed it to her father.

"What's it say, Daddy?" she asked.

"It says:

SOPHIE

Many happy returns of Christmas Day

Love from Aunt Al."

Aunt Al was Sophie's Great-great-aunt Alice, who was nearly eighty-one years old and lived in the Highlands of Scotland. She had come to lunch one day in the summer, and she and Sophie had got on like a house on fire.

"Aren't you going to open it?" asked Sophie's mother.

"It's just a card, I expect," said Sophie, but inside the envelope was another smaller envelope marked FARM MONEY and inside that was a five pound note.

"Yikes!" shouted Sophie. "I could buy a hen with that, a real one, I mean!"

"April," said Mark.

"Or May," said Matthew.

"You wait till you get your real farm," said Sophie's father. "This house would be full of animals if you had your way."

After lunch, Sophie set out her model farm on the sitting-room floor. She loaded all the animals in turn on to the trailer, and then drove the tractor into the yard to unload and arrange them.

"You're lucky," she said, holding up the turkey-cock. "We've just been eating one of your lot. Mind you, when I have real turkeys on my farm, I shan't eat any of them."

"You going to be a vegetarian?" asked her mother.

"No," said Sophie, "but you can't eat your friends. I shall eat a stranger – from the supermarket."

"This farm of yours is just going to be a collection of pets," said her father, yawning in his armchair.

"That's right," said Sophie. "I like pets. I wish I had a pet, now."

"You're much too young."

"I'm five."

"That's much too young," said the twins.

"I'll buy myself a pet, with Aunt Al's money."

"Don't be silly," said her father sleepily.

"I'm not silly."

"You are," said Matthew.

"I'm not."

"You can't eat your friends," said Sophie.
"I shall eat a stranger from the supermarket."

"You are," said Mark.

"I AM NOT."

"Be quiet, Sophie," said her mother, "and play with your toy farm. Daddy wants a nap."

Sophie put the turkey-cock down (on the duck pond, as it happened) and stamped out of the room. Hands rammed deep into the pockets of her jeans, she plodded out into the wintry garden, a short stocky figure whose dark hair looked, as always, as though she had just come through a hedge backwards. Her head was bent, there was a scowl on her round face, and as she walked along the path beside the garden wall, she mouthed the phrase that she always used to describe those who upset her.

"Mowldy, stupid and assive!" she muttered. "That's what they all are, mowldy, stupid and assive. Why can't I have a real live animal of my own – now?"

"Nee-ow?" said a voice above her head, and, looking up, Sophie saw a cat sitting on the wall. It was a jet-black cat with huge round orange eyes that stared down at her, and again it said, more confidently, "Nee-ow!"

Then it jumped down, trotted up to her with its tail held stiffly upright, and began to rub itself against her legs, purring like a steam-engine.

Sophie's frown gave way to a huge grin as she stroked the gleaming sable fur. "Happy Christmas, my dear!" she said. "And how beautiful you are! I wonder who you belong to?"

"Yee-ew!" said the cat.

At least that's how it sounded to Sophie.

*"You come along with me, my dear," said Sophie,
"and we'll see what we can find."*

IN WHICH TOM
DISAPPEARS

Sophie's first thought was to fetch the cat
something to eat. All animals must be
regularly fed, she knew, and this one was
sure to be hungry even though it looked so
sleek and healthy. Anyway it was Christmas
Day, when everybody eats more than they
should.

"So you come along with me, my dear,"
said Sophie, "and we'll see what we can
find."

She glanced at the sitting-room window,
but no one was looking out. They were all
used to Sophie's tantrums, which did not
really last long and were best left to blow
themselves over. So she plodded round to

the back of the house and in through the door that led to the kitchen. The cat followed close at heel, just as though it had been following Sophie all its life and just as though it knew what would happen next. It watched as Sophie opened the door of the fridge, and pulled some bits of skin from the remains of the turkey. She put them on a saucer, with half a leftover chipolata and some bits of bacon rind that her mother had put aside for the bird-table.

"Help yourself," she said to the black cat. "Whatever-your-name-is." She watched it eating.

"Actually," she said, "you'd better have a name, hadn't you? Trouble is, I don't know if you're a boy or a girl, and you can't tell me, can you?"

"Nee-o," said the cat, raising its head from the empty saucer.

"I think you're a boy," said Sophie, "because you're greedy. So I shall call you Tom." She took a milk bottle from the fridge and poured some into the saucer and some into a glass.

"Cheers, Tom!" said Sophie, and they both drank.

Her mother came into the kitchen.

"Sophie!" she said. "What on earth are you doing?"

"I'm giving my cat a drink of milk," said Sophie, reasonably.

"Your cat?"

"He says he's mine," said Sophie.

"Oh don't be silly. It probably belongs to the people next door. No, come to think of it, they don't have a cat. It must be a stray."

"What's a stray?"

"A cat or a dog that's lost or hasn't got a home."

"Well, this one can't be a stray, Mummy," said Sophie, "because he's got a home."

"Where?"

"Here."

"Oh no he hasn't, my girl," said Sophie's mother firmly. "That cat goes straight out of this house, now, d'you understand? Daddy doesn't like cats, you know that. Anyway it does not belong to you, it's got a perfectly good owner somewhere, and it will make its way back to its own house."

"How can he?" said Sophie. "He's lost. You said so."

The milk finished, the black cat rubbed its purring way around Sophie's mother's ankles, and automatically she bent to stroke it.

"I'm sorry, puss," she said, "but out you must go, and that is definite."

"Black cats are lucky," said Sophie.

"Out!"

"Specially if they come to you from the right-hand side. Aunt Al told me that. And Tom did."

"Do as I say, Sophie. Take that cat outside," said Sophie's mother, bracing herself for a tantrum.

To her surprise, Sophie simply said, "OK, I'll just put my wellies on and my coat – it's cold outside." When she had done so, she regarded her mother with a look of deep disapproval and added, "It's cold for cats too," and marched out, Tom following.

At the bottom of the garden was an old potting-shed, where Sophie kept her flocks and herds – of such animals, that is, as she was allowed to own.

These included woodlice, centipedes, earthworms, earwigs, slugs and snails,

The black cat hesitated on the threshold.

which lived in a variety of boxes, tins and jars. Most were allowed to come and go as they pleased, and most went, but Sophie continually replaced the losses.

Now, out of sight of the house, Sophie opened the potting-shed door and went in. The black cat hesitated on the threshold, but then, with the curiosity of all his kind, walked in. He jumped up on a large cardboard box – on the side of which was printed in black letters BAKED BEANS – sat down on the word SNALES, written in big red capitals, and proceeded to wash his face.

Sophie stood watching him. She was rubbing the tip of her nose, a sure sign of deep thought, and then she said, "I've got it! Listen, Tom, you can stay here for a bit. I'll bring you food – I bring cornflakes and biscuit crumbs and cabbage leaves for these animals anyway, so no one will notice. And you'll be quite safe – nobody comes down here in the winter – and I'll make you a nice warm bed."

First she closed the door and then she took a wooden seed tray off a shelf and lined it with an old sack. Then she lifted the black cat, with difficulty for he was quite heavy, and put him on the sack. But, with the contrariness of all his kind, he got out again, and stood by the closed door, mewing.

"I'm sorry, my dear," said Sophie firmly, "but here you must stay, and that is definite. Now out of the way, please." But, with the disdain for authority of all his kind, the cat took no notice, continuing to mew at the door.

Sophie however was more than a match for him in determination.

"Do as I say, Tom," she ordered, and when he did not move, she picked him up, plonked him down facing the wrong way, and was out of the potting-shed and had shut the door, before he could do anything about it.

At tea-time, they started by pulling the crackers and putting on paper hats. Then Sophie's father said, "What's this I hear about you bringing some stray cat into the house? Where is it now?"

Sophie disapproved of telling lies, and she had no intention of revealing the truth, so she said nothing.

"It's no good sulking," said her father

"I am not sulking."

"She took it out into the garden," her mother said. "It will have gone by now."

"Good," said her father. "You know I don't like cats."

"What sort of cat was it?" said Matthew,

taking a huge bite of Christmas cake.

"A black one."

"Boy or girl?" said Mark, doing the same.

"Boy."

"How d'you know?" chorused the twins, with their mouths full.

"Because he bolts his food like you," said Sophie. "Boys are greedier than girls, everyone knows that."

She cut off a very small bit of cake.

"You should chew each mouthful thirty-two times," she said, and popped it in.

Like a pair of hawks, the twins watched the seemingly endless movement of her jaw, and the moment she swallowed, they shouted, "That was thirty-seven times!"

"Don't tease, boys," said their mother. "You know Sophie can only count to twenty."

Sophie was still sitting at the table when

the rest of the family had finished tea. They supposed that it was the chewing that was taking her so long. But as soon as they had left the room, Sophie bolted what was on her plate, and then took off her paper hat and quickly wrapped up some leftovers in it. Carrying this parcel of food, she let herself out of the back door and plodded off down the twilit garden.

She opened the door of the potting-shed a crack and called, "Tom! Here's your supper." But there was no mew from the dark interior.

Sophie opened the door a little wider and poked her head round. There was just enough light left to see the shapes of the boxes, tins and jars that housed her flocks and herds, and the sack-covered seed tray that was to have been Tom's bed. But there was no sign of the black cat himself.

*Sophie found a gap just wide enough
for a prisoner to escape.*

Down on hands and knees, to make sure he wasn't hiding behind something, Sophie found a gap in the boards at the back where the wood was rotten, a gap just wide enough for a prisoner to escape.

Sophie felt terribly disappointed and sad. She had been so sure, in the short time that she had known the black cat, that theirs was a special sort of friendship, yet he had deserted her.

Some children might have given way to tears, but Sophie did not approve of crying. She was determined to look on the bright side. Tom had just gone for a walk. He would come back. He would need his supper.

She found a shallow flowerpot and tipped into it the mess of cake and marzipan and icing sugar and currant bun and marmite sandwich that she had brought. She filled a biscuit tin from the old water can which she kept there for dampening her slugs with. Finally she propped the door of the potting-shed ajar. Plodding back up the garden, Sophie called, "Tom! Tom! Where are you?" but there was no answer.

Early on a wet Boxing Day morning, Sophie went down to the shed, more than half hoping to find the black cat sheltering there. But a peep round the door showed only a fat mouse sitting in the flowerpot eating Christmas cake, and throughout the rest of the holidays there was no sign of Tom.

Sophie played happily enough with her toy farm, and only her mother wondered why she was quieter than usual. No one else noticed, for Sophie's father was back at work after the break, and Matthew and Mark were, as ever, perfectly content with each other's company.

It must be the prospect of starting school, her mother decided, that was making Sophie more than usually silent and solitary, spending so much time staring out into the garden. She was worried about meeting a lot of strange children – that must be it.

"You'll like school, you know," she said.

"I know," said Sophie. "I'm looking forward to it. They'll have Farming Lessons." She still firmly believed this, even though the twins had rolled their eyes and tapped their foreheads when she mentioned it.

Her mother paused in the task of trying to make some sort of order of Sophie's dark mop of unruly hair.

"You're not worried about anything, are you, darling?" she asked.

Sophie rubbed the tip of her nose.

"Only about Tom," she said after a while.

"Who's Tom?"

"My cat. You know."

"Oh, he'll be all right. Cats are good at looking after themselves."

"I wish I could have looked after him," Sophie said.

On the morning of the last Saturday of the holidays, Sophie had just finished a game of Happy Families with her father and her brothers, who had all agreed, rather unhappily, to play with her. She was driving her cows in for milking, when her mother returned from some shopping and stood, on Sophie's right, looking down at the array of toy animals.

"School on Monday," she said.

"Yes," said Sophie. "I can do the morning milking before I go and the afternoon milking when I get back."

136

Her mother handed her something wrapped in a little twist of paper.

"What is it?" said Sophie.

"Just a little present. To bring you luck."

Sophie undid it.

It was a tiny model cat, a black one, with big orange eyes.

"Why," said Sophie, "do I have to wear a skirt?"

IN WHICH SOPHIE
GOES TO SCHOOL

Every day of the two years that the twins had been at school, Sophie had always gone too, walking down with her mother or, if the weather was horrible, going in the car. But now, for the first time, she would not walk or ride home again at a quarter to nine in the morning.

Now, at last, she was a schoolgirl.

The day had not started well.

"Why," said Sophie, "do I have to wear a skirt?"

"It's part of the school uniform," her mother said. "You can't go dressed as you like."

Sophie's usual clothes consisted of an old blue jersey with her name written on it in white letters, old jeans and, most of the time, wellies.

But this morning she stood in front of the looking-glass and saw a distinctly grumpy figure wearing a grey pleated skirt and, under a maroon cardigan, a grey shirt with a striped tie.

"These clothes are mowldy, stupid and assive!" she said.

"You look very smart," her mother said.

"You look very smart," her father said when she came down to breakfast. The twins said nothing (because they had been told to say nothing), but they looked at Sophie, and then looked at one another, and grinned. Sophie eyed their grey trousers darkly.

"It's a pity you're not Scotch boys," she said.

"Why?"

"Then you'd have to wear skirts. They do. Aunt Al told me."

When they arrived at the school, Matthew and Mark galloped off without a backward look. Sophie and her mother made their way to the reception classroom. Heie they found a number of other children who were starting school for the first time. Most were clinging tightly to their mothers, some were snivelling, and one little boy was wailing loudly.

Sophie's mother glanced anxiously at her, but her daughter's only reaction was to pull down her dark eyebrows in a frown of disapproval.

"Fancy crying!" said Sophie.

"Let's hang up your anorak," said her mother. "There are some pegs in the corridor outside. Let's see if we can find yours."

If there was one word that Sophie was confident of reading it was her own name, and she had no trouble in spotting it. Beside each peg a child's name was printed on a picture of an animal – a lion, an elephant, a parrot, a rabbit. Sophie's picture was of a black-and-white cow with a big udder.

"Yikes!" said Sophie softly. "They knew!"

Sophie's mother felt that this might be a good moment to slip away. She kissed her, and said, a little tremulously, "See you later."

"Alligator," said Sophie in her usual no-nonsense way, and plodded back into the classroom.

It just so happened that the reception class teacher was also beginning her first term at the school, so that all the children, new and old alike, were strange to her.

Mostly they were strange to Sophie too, as she sat where she had been told to sit and stared stonily at the others. Suddenly her expression changed from one of suspicion to one of active dislike.

Sitting on the other side of the room was a pretty little girl with golden hair done in bunches that were tied with ribbon. This child, whose name was Dawn, Sophie had met once before and an unhappy meeting it had been.

Dawn had been invited round to Sophie's house to play, and had deliberately squashed one of Sophie's largest woodlice. In return, Sophie had taken Dawn's toy pony, a pink pony with a long silvery mane and tail, called Twinkletoes, and had jumped up and down on it until it was a dirty squashed lump whose toes would never twinkle again.

Now, unaware of Sophie's sultry glare, Dawn chattered brightly with her friends, until the teacher called for quiet. Then she told the new children that each of them would have an older child in the class to look after them until they knew their way around the school.

"I know my way round," said Sophie.

"Do you?" said the teacher. "How clever of you … let me see, you are…?"

"Sophie."

"How clever of you, Sophie. I expect you have an older sister in one of the other classes?"

"No."

"An older brother then?"

"No."

Sophie loved guessing games.

"Go on," she said. "Try again."

"She's got *two* older brothers," piped up

Unaware of Sophie's sultry glare,
Dawn chattered brightly with her friends.

Dawn. "They're twins."

Sophie glowered furiously at her, but the teacher only said, "It's Dawn, isn't it? Yes, well, you seem to know all about Sophie's family, so you can look after her."

"Yuk!" said Sophie, folding her arms and sticking out her lower lip, while the smug smile on Dawn's pretty little face vanished abruptly.

When the bell rang for morning break, the teacher made sure that each new child had its escort before letting them go. Dawn, carrying a new blue pony, stood nervously before Sophie.

"D'you want to go to the toilet?" she said.

"No," said Sophie.

She did – like mad – but she had already determined that she would do nothing that Dawn suggested.

Out in the playground, the whole school ran screaming and yelling and skipping and jumping. The twins came to make sure (because they had been told to make sure) that Sophie was not unhappy.

They found her standing in a corner, glowering at the madding crowd. Nearby, but not too near, stood her minder, Dawn.

"You OK?" shouted Mark, and, "You all right?" yelled Matthew.

Sophie nodded. Her expression, which was funereal, did not change.

The twins looked at Dawn, who was anxiously clutching the blue pony.

"What do you want?" they said together.

"I'm s'posed to be looking after her," Dawn said.

"She your friend?" said Matthew to Sophie.

"No."

"D'you want her hanging round?" said Mark.

"No."

"Well, get lost!" they both shouted, and off Dawn ran.

Sophie began to jig from foot to foot.

Her brothers regarded her with practised eyes.

"D'you want to go?" asked Mark.

"Yes."

"D'you know where to go?" asked Matthew.

"Yes."

"Well, go then!" they both said, and off Sophie ran.

One of the Bad Things that had worried Sophie about Going to School had been Having to Eat School Lunches, especially pilchards in tomato sauce which she hated, and at lunch-time she plodded into the hall feeling sure that, today of all days, it would be pilchards. To her great delight, it was sausages and chips and baked beans, followed by apple crumble and custard, both favourites of hers; and not even having to sit next to Dawn stopped her from enjoying her lunch very much.

From then on everything seemed to improve, for in the afternoon they drew pictures to take home and show their parents.

Sophie loved drawing. She worked away with her coloured felt pens, dark head bent, tongue sticking out with the effort. All the other children in the class drew pictures of their mothers or fathers, or sometimes of their houses, but Sophie's was quite different from the rest.

"What a lot of things you're putting in

your picture, Sophie," said the teacher when she came round to have a look. "What is it meant to be?"

Sophie looked at her scornfully.

"Can't you see?" she said.

"Well, I wasn't quite sure…"

"I'll show you," said Sophie, and with a red felt pen she wrote across the top of the picture in big wobbly capitals:

MY FARM

"That's *very* good, Sophie," said the teacher. "Fancy you being able to write like that, and spell correctly too! You're a bright one! D'you think you'll be a writer when you grow up?"

"Of course not," said Sophie. "I'm going to be a lady farmer."

"What have you got there, Sophie?" said her mother when she came to collect her. Sophie was carrying her drawing rolled into a scroll, with an elastic band round it.

"I did a picture," she said.

"Can I see?"

"When we get home, Mummy," Sophie said. "It's a present, you see. For you. And Daddy. And Matthew and Mark, I suppose."

"What's it of?" asked the twins.

"My farm."

"Your toy farm?"

"No, my real one, that I'm going to buy with my Farm Money, when I'm a grown-up lady."

At home Sophie would not undo the scroll, but waited till her father had come home from work. Then the whole family gathered round the kitchen table for the

The whole family gathered round the kitchen table
for the Exhibition of Sophie's Picture.

Exhibition of Sophie's Picture, the result of her labours on her first day at school.

"That's very good, Sophie," said her father. " 'My Farm', eh?"

"No, mine," said Sophie.

"I was just reading out what you had written."

"It's beautiful," said her mother doubtfully.

But the twins were not prepared to leave it at that. They knew all about the animals that Sophie proposed to have, and they demanded to be shown the whereabouts in the picture of Blossom and April and May and Shorty and Measles the pig.

There seemed, however, to be a great many more animals in the picture than these – dozens in fact, though it was anybody's guess which of the squiggly little figures were cows and which hens or horses or pigs.

"What are those?" asked Matthew, pointing to a group in one corner.

"Pigs of course," said Sophie.

"They look more like sheep," said Mark.

"Sophie's an impressionist," said her father, "and it's a great picture. But you seem to have got an awful lot of animals on your farm, considering that you're planning to begin with just those five. How will you manage that?"

"I'll breed them of course," said Sophie. "Farm animals have lots of babies. I should have thought you'd have known that."

"Yes. How silly of me."

"What's this little black thing here?" asked her mother, pointing.

"That's Tom."

"Your cat?"

"Yes."

"And what's this brown thing over here?" said Mark. "Like a heap of something."

"It is a heap of something," said Sophie. "It's the dung-heap."

"Look," said Matthew. "There's a pair of legs sticking out of the top of it, as though someone had fallen in it head first."

"They have," said Sophie. "That's Dawn."

*Dawn soon gave way to the disapproval
of the twins and the dislike of Sophie.*

IN WHICH DUNCAN
COMES TO TEA

Dawn soon gave way to the disapproval of the twins and the dislike of Sophie. She sat by her charge or lined up beside her when she was told, but otherwise she steered well clear.

Sophie for her part was already looking forward to the time, some two years ahead, when she would be a Junior and could thus do Judo. She would throw Dawn down on the mat with a terrible crash.

When the term was a fortnight old, the headmistress was talking to the reception teacher about the new intake, asking how they were getting on.

"What about the twins' sister, Sophie?" she said.

"Small but very determined," was the reply.

"How does she get on with the other children?"

"She didn't seem to think much of any of them to start with. I paired her off with Dawn, but that doesn't seem to have been a good move."

"Bit of a loner, is she?"

"She does rather keep herself to herself."

Sophie's mother was also worried.

"I know you don't like Dawn," she said, "but what about the other girls in your class?"

"Don't like any of them."

"The boys then?"

"They're silly."

"All of them?"

"Duncan's all right."

Duncan, Sophie's mother found out later, was a very small boy, the smallest of all the children in Sophie's class. Sophie, she was told on asking the teacher, made use of him at playtime. Each held one end of a skipping-rope, and then Sophie would stand still while Duncan moved in a circle around her.

"I was on playground duty today, watching them," the teacher said, "and she says to him 'Walk on!' and 'Trot!' and 'Whoa!' just as though she was lunging a pony."

Shorty! thought Sophie's mother.

Indeed when Duncan was pointed out to her, she could see that he might well have Shetland blood in his veins. He had a shaggy mane of ginger hair, short legs and a fat stomach.

Not long after that, Sophie came home with another farmyard drawing. It was much the same as the original, including the little black figure of the cat Tom, but this time there were no legs sticking out of the dung-heap. Instead, there was a short matchstick figure standing beside it.

"Who's that?" her mother asked.

"That's my farm labourer. He's chucking the cow-muck on the heap."

"What's he called?"

"Duncan."

Sophie's new friend (or more properly, it seemed, her slave, since he instantly obeyed every order that she gave him) had of course been spotted by the twins.

"Sophie's got a boy-friend," said Matthew that evening.

"Called Duncan," said Mark.

"He is not my boy-friend," said Sophie. "I've told him he can come to work for me. On my farm. When we are grown-ups."

"And what did he say to that?" asked Sophie's father.

"He said he would, of course."

"Of course. But how will you afford to pay him?"

"I shan't."

"You mean he won't get any wages?" He'll have to work for nothing?"

"Not for nothing," Sophie said. "He'll get his food. I've told him he can have free milk from my cows and free eggs from my hens and free cornflakes from my corn."

"Lucky boy!"

"He is," said Sophie. "I've told him so."

At half-term, Duncan came to tea. Sophie had told him to ask his mummy if he could, so of course he did; and then the two mothers fixed it up between them, mindful of Sophie's instructions that he should bring his

*"You have to be firm with earwigs," Sophie said.
"Don't stand any nonsense."*

wellies and that there should be crumpets and chocolate Swiss roll.

Before tea, she took him down to the potting-shed to show him her flocks and herds. She was a little disappointed that he seemed nervous of them, especially the earwigs.

"They bite," Duncan said.

"Load of rubbish," Sophie said. "No good being scared of animals if you're going to be a farm labourer."

She picked one out of the shoe box labelled YEAR WIGS.

"You have to be firm with them," she said. "Don't stand any nonsense."

She pointed to the sack-covered seed tray.

"That's my cat's bed," she said. "He's called Tom. He's very big and black."

Duncan did not look too happy at this news.

"Where is he?" he said.

"Oh, somewhere about," said Sophie, airily.

She did not notice that Duncan shot anxious glances around him as they made their way up the darkening garden. But no one could fail to notice that he enjoyed his tea. As well as the crumpets and the chocolate Swiss roll, there were sandwiches and biscuits and a fruit cake, and the budding farm worker ploughed his way through the lot.

"He'll be sick," whispered Matthew.

"Or burst," whispered Mark.

"He's going to be ever so expensive for Sophie to feed," they said to one another.

Duncan was still eating when everyone else had finished, and might, it seemed, have gone on for ever had Sophie not told him to get down, they were going to play with her toy farm, he must do the milking.

Later, when Duncan's mother had come to collect him, they were standing at the front door, waving goodbye, when suddenly there was a terrible racket somewhere in the depths of the dark garden. It was a horrible yarring, yowling, whining, wailing chorus of dreadful voices, competing, it seemed, to see who could make the most awful noise.

"Yikes!" cried Sophie. "Whatever's that?"

"Cats, fighting," said her mother.

"It might be Tom!" Sophie said, and ran inside for a torch.

Though she would not have admitted it, Sophie felt a bit scared as she crossed the lawn, shining her torch about, for it was very dark and the caterwauling was very eerie.

Suddenly there was an explosion of spitting and snarling, and in the torchlight

In the torchlight Sophie saw three dark shapes rush across the grass.

Sophie saw no less than three dark shapes rush across the grass, over the wall and away. All cats are grey at night, they say, but one of the shapes, Sophie was almost sure, looked really black.

"Tom!" she called. "Tom!" But the garden was silent now.

Not till Sophie had plodded back across the lawn and gone indoors did a distant voice answer.

"Yee-es?" it said enquiringly, but Sophie had shut the door.

*As soon as Sophie woke, she jumped out
of bed and went to her window.*

IN WHICH AUNT AL
HAS AN IDEA

"Why were those cats making all that row?"
Sophie asked later.

"Two toms, fighting, I expect," her father
said.

"There's only one Tom – my one."

"All male cats are called toms."

"Why were they fighting?"

"Over a female, I should say."

"I bet my Tom won."

"I've told you before," her mother said.
"He's not yours."

As soon as Sophie woke next morning, she
jumped out of bed and went to her window.
It was barely light, but she could see that

there was a black cat sitting in the middle of the lawn, looking up at her window with his orange eyes.

Sophie crept downstairs and opened the back door, stuffing her feet into wellies. She hurried round to the lawn but the cat had gone.

"Tom, Tom," she called, keeping her voice down so as not to wake the rest of the family, and to her joy a voice answered, "Yee-es?" or that's how it sounded to Sophie. Out of the shrubbery he came to be stroked, and then he followed her back into the kitchen.

"Have some milk, my dear," Sophie said, and filled a saucer, which Tom quickly emptied.

"Now listen, Tom," said Sophie. "You can't stay in the house, they'd only get angry, so I'll have to put you out again. But come back tomorrow morning and I'll give you some more milk, understand?"

"Yee-es," said the cat.

And indeed it seemed he did, for from now on he was waiting at the back door every morning.

"It's a funny thing," said Sophie's mother at breakfast one day, "but we seem to be using much more milk than usual. I keep having to ask the milkman for extra. Are you boys drinking more than you ordinarily do?"

"No," said the twins. "We don't much like the stuff, you know that, Mum."

"Sophie?"

Sophie stuck rigidly to the truth.

"I like milk," she said. "That's partly why I'm going to be a lady farmer. But I'm not drinking more than usual."

All might have been well, had not Sophie's father needed to go to Scotland on business.

"Sophie, get that animal out of here this minute!"

This meant catching an early train, and Tom was just enjoying his saucerful and Sophie was enjoying watching him, when her father came into the room.

"So that's where the extra milk is going!" he said. "Sophie, get that animal out of here this minute!"

"But Daddy…"

"No buts. Out!"

"Come, Tom," said Sophie with dignity. "Daddy doesn't like cats."

"I certainly don't like somebody else's cat drinking our milk," said her father. "Cats are only good for one thing and that's catching mice. That cat does not come into this house again, Sophie, d'you understand?"

"Never?" said Sophie.

She looked so woebegone that her father relented a little.

"I'll tell you what," he said, "if ever anyone sees a mouse in this house, then we'll think about having a cat."

"And don't think you can go putting saucers of milk out in the garden, Sophie," said her mother later, when she had heard all about it. "Cats should be given water to drink anyway, milk just makes them fat. And that cat's fat enough already." She should have known that Sophie, though small, was very determined, and if she had been about early enough in the days that followed, she would have seen that Sophie had no intention of giving Tom up. She did not let him in, and she did not give him milk, but she saw to it that there were scraps of some sort put out for his breakfast every morning.

Soon it was plain that Tom had forsaken his owners, whoever they were. Whether they were unworried by his disappearance, or whether they had moved house or gone to another district or abroad, no one ever knew, but the black cat had clearly adopted Sophie's garden as his territory and Sophie as his mistress. Now he even slept in the potting-shed.

Sophie was delighted of course. If only Daddy liked cats, she thought. If only we had mice in the house. But it was lovely to be continually meeting Tom in the garden, and lovely to be in bed at night and think of her black cat hunting in the black night outside.

"I bet Aunt Al will like you," she said to Tom. "Daddy's bringing her back with him, for a visit, when he comes home from Scotland. She lives in the Highlands, you know. They have Wild Cats there. Would you like to meet a Wild Cat?"

"Nee-o," said Tom.

When Aunt Al did arrive, apparently as fresh as a daisy after so long a journey, Sophie lost no time.

"Come and see Tom, Aunt Al," she said.

Aunt Al, small and birdlike with a sharp beaky nose, looked at Sophie with her head on one side.

"Who's Tom?" she said. "Your boy-friend?"

"No, that's Duncan," said Matthew.

"Tom's a cat," said Mark.

Aunt Al turned to her great-nephew.

"I thought you didn't like cats," she said.

"I don't," said Sophie's father. "And it is not allowed in the house."

"It's a stray," said Sophie's mother. "It seems to have adopted us. I've rung the police and the RSPCA but no one has claimed it."

Aunt Al, small and birdlike, looked at
Sophie with her head on one side.

"They have," said Sophie. "I have. It's my cat."

Tom seemed to take to Aunt Al straightaway. He came out of the shrubbery and wrapped himself around her thin bird's legs and made his steam-engine noise. Aunt Al scratched the roots of his ears.

"So you can't come indoors?" she said.

"Nee-o," said Tom.

"Only if we have a mouse in the house, Daddy says," said Sophie.

"Which is highly unlikely, I suppose," said Aunt Al.

The very next day was one of those lovely mild early spring days full of promise, and in the afternoon Aunt Al and Sophie were walking round the garden together. Sophie was carrying the yellow bucket in which she collected fresh creatures for her flocks and herds, to replace those who had decided to leave.

They came to the potting-shed, and there inside was Tom, crouching low.

"He's caught something," Aunt Al said, and sure enough there was a mouse between his forepaws, perhaps the same fat mouse that Sophie had found eating Christmas cake. It was alive and, though bedraggled, apparently unharmed, but every time it tried to crawl away, Tom raked it back.

"Poor mouse!" Sophie cried. "Leave it, Tom!" But the black cat only growled at her.

"Cats eat mice, you know," said Aunt Al. "It's quite natural. He won't let you take it away from him."

"He will!" said Sophie. "I'll make him!" and she moved towards him in a most determined manner, swinging her yellow bucket threateningly.

With a cry that sounded remarkably like "Yikes!" Tom shot out of the shed.

"We can't just leave it here," said Sophie, looking at the mouse, so shocked that it was too afraid to move. "Tom will come back. What shall we do, Aunt Al?"

"Hang on half a tick," said Aunt Al. "Got an empty box somewhere? I've just had a brilliant idea."

Thus it was that, later on, Sophie and her mother and her great-great-aunt were having tea in the kitchen, when Aunt Al suddenly said, "What was that?"

"What was what?" said Sophie's mother.

"I thought I heard a little scratching noise. As though there was a mouse somewhere in the room."

*With a cry that sounded remarkably
like "Yikes!" Tom shot out of the shed.*

"There are no mice in this house," said Sophie's mother. "I can tell you that for sure."

"I'm certain I heard it," said Aunt Al. "Listen, there it is again!"

"It's over in that corner," Sophie said. "Somewhere by that old cardboard box."

Sophie's mother got up from the table and went over to the box and lifted the lid. Then she shut it again quickly.

"Oh!" she cried. "It is a mouse! Oh, I don't like mice! Sophie, take it out into the garden."

When Sophie had done as she was told, she plodded back into the kitchen.

"Mummy," she said. "I told you what Daddy said, didn't I?"

"What?"

"'If ever anyone sees a mouse in this house,' he said, 'we'll think about having a

182

cat.' So when Daddy comes back from work we can tell him we've seen a mouse, can't we?" Sophie's mother looked at them both, the five year old and the eighty-one year old. Their faces were expressionless.

Hers broke into a big smile.

"You wicked pair!" she said.

*It was plain to everyone that, now and
for ever, he was Sophie's Tom.*

IN WHICH DAWN
TAKES A TUMBLE

Tom proved himself to be a very tactful animal. He was careful not to take advantage of his new position as a house cat. He did not mew to be let in or out, he did not claw at curtains, or jump on chair covers with dirty feet, or worse. He did not make a nuisance of himself in any way.

He steered well clear of Sophie's father as though aware of his distaste for cats, and he kept away from the twins, suspecting that they might tease him. He was polite to Sophie's mother, but it was plain to everyone that, now and for ever, he was Sophie's Tom.

Sophie, on the other hand, was not a tactful person. Not content with being allowed to have Tom indoors, she demanded that he sleep on her bed.

"No," her mother said firmly. "Don't push your luck, Sophie. Daddy's being very good about all this, he's even having a cat-flap put in the back door; and I'm buying the tinned meat for Tom, and that's quite enough to be going on with."

Sophie, however, got her way in an unexpected fashion.

About a week after Aunt Al's visit, Sophie came home from school saying that her head itched.

"Whereabouts?" her mother asked.

"Everywhere in my hair," said Sophie, scratching away in her dark mop.

"Head lice, I expect," said Matthew.

"Or fleas from the cat," said Mark, and they beat a hasty retreat.

Later, when Sophie was in the bath, her mother noticed that there were spots on her back, dark, pink, flat spots, and she called the doctor.

"Keep her in bed for a while," the doctor said. "She's got a bit of a temperature. It's chicken-pox."

"I haven't been near any chickens," Sophie said.

The doctor laughed.

"Try to stop her scratching the spots," he said to Sophie's mother. "Anything you can think of to distract her? What does she specially like doing?"

"Drawing," said her mother.

"And playing with my cat," said Sophie.

"Good," said the doctor. "Well, you stay in bed for a couple of days, and have your cat with you, and then you can draw her."

"Him," said Sophie. "Bring Tom, please, Mummy."

"Only in the daytime," Sophie's mother said when the doctor had gone. "This cat goes outside at night."

But that didn't last long either. Sophie always left her bedroom door open, and Tom came in through the cat-flap as and when he pleased and sneaked upstairs like a shadow. And a rather fat shadow too – he was getting positively tubby. Sophie woke each morning to feel the warm weight of him on her feet.

Apart from sitting for his portrait dozens of times, Tom proved a blessing during Sophie's chicken-pox, for, whenever she felt she *must* scratch her spots they itched so much, she scratched Tom instead, and that of course he much enjoyed.

Meanwhile, at school, several other children in Sophie's class had caught chicken-pox, though not, Sophie would have been sorry to hear, Dawn.

Dawn, moreover, was not slow to take advantage of Sophie's absence. She had not forgotten or forgiven the squashing of Twinkletoes, and now she quite deliberately set out to ensnare Sophie's future farm labourer. It was not difficult, for Duncan was not only a biddable little boy but very greedy. Regular offers of sweets from Dawn quickly made him her slave, and he followed her about with the same dog-like devotion he had once shown to Sophie.

Dawn should have known better. Setting herself up against Sophie was rather like a toy poodle challenging a bulldog, and she lived to regret it.

At morning break on her first day back at

school, Sophie went out into the play-ground carrying her skipping-rope. Part of the game she had invented, with herself as horse-breaker, was to go out into the paddock (the playground) and call the pony (Duncan). Then, when he came obediently trotting up, she would attach the lunge (the skipping-rope) to his harness (hand), and the training would begin.

Now she plodded out again into the noisy throng of children and called "Duncan! Duncan! Come up, come up, good boy!"

She had trained him to whinny in reply to this summons, but now she heard no answer. Then she saw, at the far end of the playground, a sight to make her blood boil. It was Dawn, lunging Duncan! In her left hand she held the blue toy pony, in her right the end of a skipping-rope, while Duncan marched solemnly around her.

Sophie plodded across the playground and stood, just outside Duncan's circle, and glowered at Dawn.

"What are you doing with my pony?" she said.

Dawn waved the blue toy.

"It's not yours," she said, "it's mine, and don't you touch it or I'll tell Miss."

"I don't mean that pony," said Sophie.

Duncan, meantime, having last received the command, "Walk on!", walked on, and since Dawn was not turning with him, for she feared to take her eyes off Sophie, he walked in ever-decreasing circles, till at last the rope was wrapped tightly round Dawn's legs and Duncan was brought to a halt. Dawn was cocooned, like a big fly parcelled up by a little spider.

Sophie stumped up to the two prisoners.

"You," she said to Dawn, "are mowldy,

*"And as for you," Sophie said
to Duncan, "you're sacked!"*

stupid and assive," and she gave her a push in the chest so that they both fell down.

Sophie listened with pleasure to their howls, and then addressed her would-be farm labourer.

"And as for you," she said, "you're sacked!"

"You should have seen it, Mum!" said the twins, when their mother came to collect the three children after school.

"Dawn was bawling her head off!" said Mark.

"And Duncan was bawling his head off!" said Matthew.

"And the teacher on duty came up..."

"And said, 'Whatever's going on?'..."

"And Dawn said, 'She pushed me'..."

"And the teacher said, 'Who pushed you?'..."

"And Dawn said, 'Sophie'..."

"And the teacher said, 'Did you, Sophie?'..."

"And Sophie said, 'Yes'..."

"And the teacher said, 'Why?'..."

"And Sophie wouldn't answer."

"So what happened then?" asked their mother.

"Sophie had to go to the headmistress," said Matthew.

"In her office," said Mark.

"And what did the headmistress say?"

"We don't know," they said. "We listened at the keyhole, but we couldn't hear."

"What did she say, Sophie?" asked her mother.

"She said I was naughty."

"And what did you say?"

"Nothing."

"So what did she do?"

"Made me stay in all of the next play-time," said Sophie.

She grinned.

"I drew a picture," she said.

She took a piece of paper out of her satchel. It was one of her standard farmyard scenes, but this time there were two pairs of legs, one long and skinny, one short and fat, sticking out of the top of the dung-heap.

*The twins' eighth birthday fell in late April, and
Sophie was busy thinking what to get them.*

IN WHICH SOPHIE
GETS A SURPRISE

The twins' eighth birthday fell in late April, and Sophie was busy thinking what to get them.

"It's difficult, you see," she said to Tom, "to know whether to buy them the same things, which is a bit boring, or different things, when one might like his present more than the other."

She stroked his fat black stomach.

"What do you think?" she said, but he only purred.

She sought her father's opinion.

"I should ask them what they want," he said. So she did.

"What would you like for your birthday,

Matthew?" she said to her elder brother.

"A radio-controlled model car," he said.

"And I want one too," said Mark.

"Oh," said Sophie. "What kind?"

"A Lamborghini," said Matthew.

"A Dune Buggy," said Mark.

"Oh," said Sophie.

"How much do they cost?" she said.

"About £50," they said.

"£50 the two?"

"No, £50 each."

"Oh," said Sophie.

She took her Farm Money out of her piggy-bank. There was Aunt Al's £5 note and quite a lot of coins that she had saved. She sought her mother's help in counting them.

"You've got 47p there," her mother said. "So that's £5.47p altogether."

"I don't think I can afford the sort of things the twins want," she said to Tom later.

"Nee-o."

"I suppose I could cut the £5 note in half."

"Nee-o."

Sophie rather agreed with him. She was not mean by nature, but that would have been over generous.

"You're right, Tom. It'll have to be the 47p. And it'll have to be sweets as usual. They like sweets."

So next time they went shopping, she told her mother that she was going to spend 47p buying sweets for the twins' birthday present.

In the shop, almost the first things to catch Sophie's eye were chocolate pennies.

"How much are those, Mummy?" she said.

Her mother looked.

"A penny each."

"So I could buy forty-seven of them?"

"Yes."

So she did.

Afterwards she said, "Mummy, what's half 47p?"

"Let's see … it's 23½ p. Only there aren't halfpennies any more. If you wanted to split it, it would have to be 24p and 23p."

"Oh blow," said Sophie. "That's no good. They must have exactly the same number of chocolate pennies."

"Take one away," said her mother. "Then there'll be twenty-three for Matthew and twenty-three for Mark."

"Take one away? But what shall I do with it?"

"Open your mouth and shut your eyes, and I'll give you something to make you wise."

*"Open your mouth and shut your eyes,
and I'll give you something to make you wise."*

After carefully dividing the chocolate pennies into two heaps (she could count to twenty-three now), Sophie had then put each heap into a little cardboard box, had written the twins' names on each box, and then put LOVE FROM SOPHIE on both. The boxes were part of a store that she kept in the potting-shed, but Matthew and Mark were not aware that they had once been used for keeping black beetles in.

When the day came, they were delighted with Sophie's presents.

"Gosh, thanks, Sophie!" they said.

"That's all right."

"Must have cost you an awful lot," they said.

"It did. 47p."

By chance the birthday was on a Sunday, which meant that the children's father was at home, and what's more, it was a beautiful sunny spring day. Matthew and Mark had each been allowed to ask three friends to tea, so they chose six boys with whom they regularly played football.

"Would you like to ask someone, Sophie?" her mother said.

"Darling Dawn?" said Mark.

"Or dearest Duncan?" said Matthew.

"Yuk!" said Sophie. "No thanks. I'll just have my friend Tom."

"You give that cat too much food," her father said. "He's as fat as butter. He needs to take more exercise. Which reminds me – boys, do you want to have the Olympic Games again?"

"Oh yes, please, Dad!" they cried.

The previous year their father, who was keen on that sort of thing, had organized all sorts of running and jumping and throwing competitions, and they had called them "the Olympic Games". There were races, short ones across the lawn and long ones right round the garden, and high jump and long jump, and throwing the discus (a tin plate) and tossing the caber (a clothes prop) and putting the shot (a brick).

So this year they did the same, and one or other of the twins, who were good at that sort of thing, won nearly everything, or else dead-heated for first place.

Sophie went in for every event and was always last because she was much the smallest, but everyone cheered her for her determination. And in the last race of all, the marathon, everyone had to run six times round the garden while Sophie was allowed to run only three times, and she won!

Then they all ate an enormous tea.

After all the guests had gone, Sophie plodded upstairs to play with her farm before bedtime. It had grown quite a bit since Christmas, for Sophie had either bought or been given a number of new animals, including a goat and some geese and a good few more cows. So big was it now that she had been allowed the use of the attic room at the top of the house so that the farm could be permanently laid out there on the floor. In the attic were some old bits of furniture and various oddments, and there was even an off-cut of carpet, grassy-green in colour, on which the animals stood or lay or grazed.

Sophie knelt on the floor, the black cat purring at her side. With one hand she stroked him, with the other she began to

"Time for milking," Sophie said.
"Time for bed," said her father.

move the dairy herd.

"Time for milking," she said.

"Time for bed," said her father's voice.

He came in and sat down in a broken armchair.

"Come on, my old farmer," he said. "You must be tired, specially after winning a marathon."

"In a minute, Daddy, I've got to get the cows in first."

She began to use both hands to pick them up, and Tom, released, jumped on to her father's lap. To her amazement, he was not only allowed to remain there, but she saw her father was actually stroking him!

"Daddy!" she said. "I thought you didn't like cats!"

"I don't," he said. "Except this one. I've got used to him, I suppose. You're a good boy, Tom, aren't you?"

"Nee-o," said the black cat.

"Oh yes, you are. Come on, Sophie love. Beddy-byes."

As soon as she woke the next morning Sophie felt that something was different. What? Oh yes, there was no black hot-water bottle on her feet. She got dressed and went out to see to her flocks and herds. There was no sign of Tom in the potting-shed, or anywhere in the garden, and stranger still, he did not appear at breakfast-time, which was when Sophie usually fed him.

By the time she had finished eating, Sophie was becoming rather worried, though she did not say anything to the others. She plodded upstairs to the attic to do the morning milking.

As she neared the door, she suddenly heard some faint little squeaks. They seemed to be coming from the old arm-chair. Sophie went to look in it, and then she gave a cry of "Yikes!"

In the chair, snuggling against the now much smaller stomach of Tom, were four little furry bodies. One was tabby, one was tortoiseshell, one was black with a white bib and white feet, and the fourth was coal-black, just like its mother.

"Oh Tom!" Sophie said. "How clever you are, my dear! And all this time I thought you were a boy. Whatever am I going to call you now?"

But the only answer was a loud proud purr of contentment from Sophie's Tom.

SOPHIE
HITS SIX

*Beano sat in the doorway
wiffling his nose madly.*

CONTENTS

"One thing's certain," said Sophie's father.
"You can't call him ... her ... Tom any more."

TOMBOY

"One thing's certain," said Sophie's father. "You can't call him ... her ... Tom any more."

Tom was Sophie's black cat, who had come from nowhere and adopted her, and had now, much to everyone's surprise, given birth to four kittens.

"Female cats are called queens," said Sophie's mother. "You could call her Queenie."

"I don't like that," said Sophie.

"How about Elizabeth?" said Matthew, who was eight, two and a half years older than Sophie and ten minutes older than his twin brother Mark.

"Why Elizabeth?"

"Well, it's the Queen's name."

"Or Diana?" said Mark.

"Why?"

"That's what the Princess of Wales is called. She'll be queen one day."

"I can't wait that long to give my cat another name," said Sophie.

The twins however, were quite taken with this idea of royalty. As often happened, they had the same thought at the same moment, and they looked at one another and grinned and said, "How about Fergie?"

"Spelt F-U-R-gie," said Sophie's father, and everyone laughed, except Sophie.

"You're all mowldy, stupid and assive!" she said, and she stumped off, hands rammed deep into the pockets of her old jeans, a frown of disapproval on her round face.

She plodded up to the attic at the top of the house, where all the animals of her toy farm were laid out. Here, in the depths of an old armchair, lay her cat, nursing the four kittens, one tabby, one tortoiseshell, one black with a white bib and white feet and one exactly like its mother, whose black coat Sophie now stroked.

"I can't call you Tom any more," she said, "because you're not one, are you, my dear?"

"Nee-o," said the cat, or that's how it sounded to Sophie.

"I suppose I could call you Thomasina, but I don't much fancy that, do you?"

"Nee-o."

"Mum and Daddy and the twins weren't any help."

Sophie rubbed the tip of her nose, a sure sign that she was thinking deeply.

*Sophie sat on the arm of the old chair,
stroking her nameless cat.*

"I wish Aunt Al was here," she said. "I bet she'd have a good idea."

Aunt Al was Sophie's father's great-aunt, and therefore Sophie's great-great-aunt. When she had first been told this, she had imagined Aunt Al as enormous, but actually she was very small, with thin legs like a bird. She was nearly eighty-two years old, and she lived in the Highlands of Scotland. She and Sophie had become great friends.

Sophie sat on the arm of the old chair, stroking her nameless cat and wondering whether to write a letter to Aunt Al.

"Trouble is," she said, "I'd have to have help with the spelling and everything, and anyway it would all take a long time."

Just then she heard the trill of the telephone downstairs, and she jumped up, grinning.

"Yikes!" said Sophie. "That's it! I'll ring her!"

Something told Sophie it might be best to say nothing to the others about this phone call. It could perhaps be rather expensive to telephone the Highlands because they were so high. If they ask me, she thought, I'll tell them I did it (for Sophie disapproved of lying), but if they don't know, they won't ask.

So she waited that afternoon, a fine Saturday afternoon in early May, until her brothers had gone off to play football (of which they never tired) with some friends, her mother had gone to do some shopping and her father was working in the garden.

Sophie found Aunt Al's number in the phone book and carefully dialled it. She heard the ringing tone, and then Aunt Al's brisk voice, as loud and clear as if she were

Sophie found Aunt Al's number in the
phone book and carefully dialled it.

in the room, saying, "Hello. Who is it?"

"It's Sophie."

"Sophie? My niece?"

"Great-great-niece, Aunt Al."

"Great-great-aunt to you. How nice to hear your voice, Sophie. Are you OK? Anything the matter?"

"Yes, there is."

"Nobody ill or anything?"

"No. It's my cat."

"Tom?"

"Yes. Well, no. You see, it's not Tom any more, because she's had four babies."

"Whew!" said Aunt Al. "Surprise, surprise."

"And so she's got to have a new name," said Sophie, "and I can't think of a good one. That's why I'm ringing you up, to ask if you can help me."

"Right," said Aunt Al. "Give me a minute."

Sophie waited, imagining, as she always did, Aunt Al sitting on top of a mountain somewhere, surrounded by golden eagles and blue hares and red deer. In a minute her voice would come whizzing down the telephone wires, down the mountainside, off the edge of the Highlands, out of Scotland, and all the way nearly to the bottom of England, all in a fraction of a second.

"Tomboy," said Aunt Al.

"What?" said Sophie. "That's even worse than plain Tom."

"No, it's not. Don't you know what a tomboy is?"

"No."

"A tomboy is a high-spirited girl that likes romping about. Your cat's high-spirited, isn't she?"

"Yes."

"Well then."

One of the reasons why Sophie and Aunt Al got on so well was that they were both direct, no-nonsense people. They did what had to be done, said what had to be said, and that was the end of it.

"OK," said Sophie. "Thanks. See you."

"Sometime in the summer, I hope," said Aunt Al, and rang off.

At tea-time Sophie said, "My cat's got her new name."

"What is it?" chorused the twins.

"Tomboy."

"What?" they said. "That's even worse than plain Tom."

"Don't they teach you anything in your class?" said Sophie scornfully. "You're ingerant, that's what you are."

"Don't you mean 'ignorant'?" said her father.

"Don't they teach you anything in your class?" said Sophie scornfully.

"That too," said Sophie.

"But Sophie," said her mother, "do you know what 'tomboy' means?"

"Of course," said Sophie. "A tomboy is a high-spirited girl that likes romping about. Can I get down please?"

"Yes," said her mother, "if you've finished. Where are you off to?"

"To feed Tomboy," said Sophie, "and to find names for my four kittens." And off she plodded.

Sophie, though small, was very determined, and a worrying thought crossed her mother's mind.

"I do hope," she said, "she doesn't think that she can keep those kittens."

"One thing's certain," said Sophie's father, "she can't. As soon as they're old enough, we must find them homes. One cat's enough, let alone five."

Up in the attic, Sophie addressed the kittens. Her firm ambition in life was to be a lady farmer, and she knew well that farmers, whether ladies or no, were always looking to increase their flocks and herds.

"Now, my dears," she said, "let's hope that you're all girls. Then, once you're big enough, you can all have babies too. And suppose each of you has four, that will make … let's see –" and Sophie began to count upon her fingers.

*"Sophie takes a lot of trouble
with her work," said the teacher.*

DOWN ON THE FARM

Sophie liked school. Learning things, she had decided by the end of her first term, was interesting, even though they did not have Farming Lessons, as she had hoped they would. But she could see that to be a lady farmer one day meant that you had to know how to read and write and do sums, so she set about these tasks in her usual determined manner.

Early in the summer term, her teacher was asked by the headmistress, "How is Sophie getting on?"

"Very well really. She takes a lot of trouble with her work. Wants to be a farmer, she tells me, so we do a lot of number work with the bottles of milk in the morning! Strange little girl though – lives in a world of her own."

"Still a bit of a loner, is she?"

"A bit. She certainly doesn't have a special friend in the class."

"Who's your special friend, Sophie?" her mother said one evening.

"Tomboy," said Sophie.

"No, I mean at school. In your class."

"Dawn?" said Matthew.

Dawn was a pretty little fair-haired girl, always beautifully dressed, the exact opposite of Sophie, both in looks and nature.

"Yuk!" said Sophie.

"Duncan?" said Mark.

Duncan was a very small, fat, short-legged boy with ginger hair. A one-time playmate of Sophie's, he had been "stolen" by Dawn while Sophie was away having chicken-pox. Both had paid dearly for this.

"He's a wally," said Sophie.

"Don't you like any of the children in your class then, Sophie?" asked her father.

"Not specially. Andrew's all right."

Her mother waited until Sophie had plodded off upstairs to play with the kittens, and then she said to the twins, "Who's Andrew?"

"He's new this term," said Mark.

"He's a farmer's son," said Matthew.

"Aha! Is he nice?"

"Dunno," they said. "We don't play with the infants."

In point of fact Sophie hadn't decided whether Andrew was nice or not – nor did she care. Once she had found out that his father was a farmer, she had determined to make a friend of him. Then, she thought, he would invite her to tea at the farm, and after a bit she would be able to go there often. She would be so useful to Andrew's father that he would ask her to come and help regularly – every day perhaps. And when she left school, she could work there. And, later, she and Andrew would probably get married and have four babies, just like Tomboy, and live happily ever after on the farm.

With such a prospect in view, what did it matter whether she liked Andrew or not?

Sophie took her time. She did not try to bribe him with sweets, as Dawn would have done, nor did she set out to boss him as she had bossed Duncan. Instead she began to ask Andrew lots of questions – about farming of course – whenever she just happened to find herself standing next to him in the playground.

Sophie's reason for this questioning was purely and simply to learn things that would be useful to her one day.

Andrew however, a sturdy little boy of about Sophie's height and build, but with very fair, almost white, hair, was flattered to be thought so knowledgeable, and answered these queries readily, if not always accurately.

"Your dad's a farmer, isn't he?" was Sophie's first question.

"Yes," said Andrew.

"I'm going to be a farmer when I grow up."

"You can't."

"Why not?"

"Farmers are men."

"Well," said Sophie, "I'm going to be a lady farmer. So there."

Andrew set off round the playground shouting,
"Broom-a-broom-a-broom-a-broom!"

"I'm going to be a man farmer."

"You're lucky," said Sophie, "living on a farm now. Has your dad got cows?"

"Yes, hundreds."

"Can you milk them?"

"Yes, 'course I can."

"What else can you do?"

"Drive a tractor," said Andrew. He gripped an imaginary steering-wheel, engaged an imaginary gear, and set off round the playground shouting, "Broom-a-broom-a-broom-a-broom!"

Sophie stood waiting until he had completed a circuit, pulled on an imaginary handbrake and switched off.

"I wish I could see your tractor," she said.

But instead of the hoped-for invitation, Andrew only said, "It's green."

"How much did it cost?"

"'Bout half a million pounds."

"Yikes!" said Sophie. "Your dad must be rich!"

"He is," said Andrew. "And I shall be too when I grow up. I shall have six tractors and I shall have cows and pigs and sheep and chickens and ducks and geese and …"

"… a Shetland pony?" said Sophie.

"Lots of them."

Each day now, at morning and afternoon playtimes, Sophie plied Andrew with questions of an agricultural nature. The fact that she monopolized his company did not escape the notice of her brothers.

Matthew and Mark prided themselves on being fast runners and, with the school's summer sports in mind, spent their time in highspeed dashes across the playground – in which, not surprisingly, they almost always deadheated. However, they could not help but see that each time they hurled themselves against the chain-link fence that acted as a finishing line, there were Sophie and Andrew, dark and fair heads together, chattering away nineteen to the dozen.

"Sophie's always talking to that Andrew," they said to their parents.

"Why ever shouldn't she?" said their mother. "It's nice she's made a special friend at last, and he's a nice-looking little boy too."

"He's not my special friend," said Sophie. "He just knows all about farming, that's all."

"Must be a clever chap," said her father. "How old is he?"

"Five."

"Fancy!"

"Sophie fancies Andrew!" chanted the twins, and they ran off before Sophie had

*"I'm not having those kittens messing
all over the attic,"* said Sophie's mother.

time to tell them that not only were they mowldy, but also both stupid and assive.

"Don't take any notice, darling," said her mother. "They're only teasing."

"It doesn't worry me," said Sophie loftily. "They only do it to be iterating."

"Don't you mean 'irritating'?" said her father.

"Both," said Sophie.

A couple of weeks went by, during which time Sophie continued her questioning. She was also made to move her own livestock from the attic to the potting-shed at the bottom of the garden.

"I'm not having those kittens messing all over the attic," her mother said.

"But they'll mess all over the potting-shed," said Sophie.

"And you'll clear it all up. That's what

*At the end of the school day Andrew's
mother saw her son approaching.*

farmers spend most of their time doing, you know – clearing up all the muck their animals make."

"Your cows must make an awful lot of cowpats," Sophie said to Andrew the next day. "I wish I could see them."

"See the cowpats?"

"No, the cows."

"You can if you like."

"You'll have to ask me to tea."

"All right."

Sophie sighed. Silly boy, she thought, I'll have to fix it all myself, I can see.

"You ask your mummy to ask my mummy if I can," she said, "and then she can bring me."

"All right."

So at the end of the school day Andrew's mother saw her son approaching, his hand firmly held by a stocky little girl with an untidy mop of dark hair and a determined expression. Sophie's mother arrived in time to hear the ensuing conversation.

"Go on, Andrew, ask her," said Sophie.

"Mum," said Andrew. "Can Sophie come to tea?"

"She'd obviously fixed the whole thing up herself," Sophie's mother said to her husband. "I'd never even met the boy's mother before, but she seemed very nice. I said we'd pick Sophie up again about six."

"She'll have got herself into a lovely mess, I shouldn't wonder."

"Oh, I don't know – I made her take her wellies."

The phone rang in the hall.

Sophie's mother came back from answering it.

"You were right," she said. "That was Andrew's mother saying could I bring some clean clothes, Sophie is absolutely filthy. She slipped up and sat down in a really squelchy cowpat."

"Ah well," said Sophie's father. "Farming's just like any other job. Start at the bottom and work up."

*Sophie decided to call the kittens
Molly, Dolly, Holly and Polly.*

BEANO

Down in the potting-shed the four kittens were growing fast. Though Sophie kept the door shut while she was at school (for fear that a Fierce Cat-eating Dog should jump into the garden and gobble them all up), there was a small hole in the boards at the back of the shed, through which Tomboy came and went at her pleasure.

Sophie liked choosing names, and, confident that the kittens were all female, had decided after much thought to call them Molly, Dolly, Holly and Polly.

"Those are all girls' names," her father said.

"They're all girls," said Sophie.

"How d'you know?"

"I just do."

"Wouldn't it be better to give them names that sound different?" her mother asked. "Those all sound the same."

"It's easy to tell them apart," Sophie said. "Molly's the tabby, Dolly's the tortoise-shell, Holly's the black-and-white one and Polly's all black."

Her mother sighed. "That's not quite what I meant," she said.

"It makes no odds," said Sophie's father. "In a couple of weeks they'll all have to go, Sophie. I hope you realize that?"

"Can't I even keep one?"

"No."

"It's not fair," said Sophie to the twins. "They won't let me keep any of the kittens."

"You've got Tomboy," said Matthew.

246

"You don't want five cats," said Mark.

"I do," said Sophie. "While I'm waiting to be a lady farmer I could be a lady cat-breeder. If I could keep Molly and Dolly and Holly and Polly and they all had babies, I could sell loads of kittens and save up loads of money for my farm." And she pointed at her piggy-bank, on whose side was stuck a notice which read:

FARM MUNNY
THANK YOU
SOPHIE

"They won't let you," said the twins.

Two weeks went by, and Sophie's father placed an advertisement in the local paper.

"Four pretty kittens," it said. "Good homes wanted."

"I wouldn't mind, if only you were boys," said Sophie as she sat on the floor of the potting-shed while the kittens played around her. "But it's such a waste. Female animals are much the most important – any farmer knows that."

Just then she heard voices, and in a moment her mother appeared in the doorway with a large tall lady.

"Ah," she said. "Here's Sophie, with her kittens. Now, was it a boy you wanted, or a girl?"

"A queen," said the large tall lady. "A female."

"These are all female, Sophie says. Can you tell?"

"Of course," said the large tall lady. "Kept cats all my life. One of these is certainly a little queen, I can tell you that straight off," and she pointed at Dolly.

"Was it a boy you wanted, or a girl?"
Sophie's mother asked the large tall lady.

"How do you know?" said Sophie's mother.

"Tortoiseshell. Torts are always female. Let's have a look at the other three ... let's see now ... you're a boy ... and you're a boy ... and you're a boy. Three little toms."

"Oh," said Sophie glumly.

"So I'll take the little tortoiseshell if I may. Does she have a name?"

"Dolly," said Sophie gloomily.

"And you're Sophie?"

Sophie nodded. Only one female, she thought, and she has to go and pick that one.

"So how much do you want for Dolly, Sophie?" asked the large tall lady.

"Excuse me," said Sophie's mother. "I can hear the phone ringing. I shan't be a minute," and out she went.

Sophie rubbed the tip of her nose. I'll say

a silly price, she thought, and then she'll say, "Oh, that's much too much," and then she won't take Dolly.

"Five pounds," she said.

The large tall lady produced her purse, and from it she took a five-pound note.

"That's fair enough," she said. "I don't believe in getting something for nothing," and she handed Sophie the money.

"And when the woman had gone off with the kitten," Sophie's mother said to her husband that evening, "I went down to the potting-shed to comfort Sophie, and, lo and behold, she'd flogged it for a fiver."

"'Farm Munny'!" said Sophie's father admiringly. "And still three to go!"

However Sophie was to find that other people were not so generous.

In the days that followed, the black-and-white kitten went to an old man who gave Sophie ten pence ("For your piggy-bank, young lady"), and the tabby to a jolly couple who gave Sophie a nice smile and a pat on the head.

Now only the black kitten remained.

"I wonder where you will go, my dear?" said Sophie sadly. Soon there would be no kittens to play with.

"You'll miss them, won't you?" said Sophie to Tomboy.

"Nee-o."

Just then Sophie heard her mother calling.

"Hurry!" she cried. "It's Aunt Al on the phone. She wants to talk to you."

Sophie galloped up the lawn.

"Hello, Aunt Al," she said breathlessly.

"You sound puffed."

"I was running."

*The tabby went to a jolly couple who gave
Sophie a nice smile and a pat on the head.*

"Tomboy's kittens. Have they all gone?"

"All but one."

"Keep it for me."

"For you?"

"Yes. My old cat's died. He was very ancient, miles older than me if you multiply by seven like you do with a dog's age. Daddy's coming up to Scotland on business next month and bringing me back to stay. D'you think you could keep your last kitten another four weeks, till I can collect it?"

"Oh yes!"

"What colour is it?"

"Black, like Tomboy."

"Lucky," said Aunt Al.

"If they come to you from the right-hand side."

"What's it called?"

"Polly."

"So it's female?"

"No, actually. I thought she was but he isn't."

"We'll have to change the name. So he gets used to a new one before I come."

"You choose then," said Sophie.

"Right," said Aunt Al. "Give me a minute."

Sophie waited, thinking of Aunt Al on her mountain and feeling very glad that the black kitten would live happily at the top of the Highlands.

"Are you still there?" said Aunt Al.

"Yes."

"Ollie. Short for Oliver."

"OK."

"How much d'you want for him?"

"Nothing."

"We'll see about that."

They sounded equally determined.

*Sophie made sure Ollie came to
Aunt Al from the right-hand side.*

"Let me speak to your mother."

"OK," said Sophie. "Here she is. See you," and she plodded off down to the potting-shed to tell the good news to Tomboy and Ollie.

Meanwhile her mother was saying on the telephone, "In exchange for the kitten, you mean? What a nice idea, Aunt Al – you know how mad about animals she is ... no, her father won't object, I'll make sure of that ... yes, we'll see about somewhere to keep it ... no, we'll keep it a secret, shan't say a word – you can spring the surprise when you come."

When Aunt Al did come, four weeks later, the very first thing she wanted to do was to see Ollie. And Sophie made sure that he came to her from the right-hand side.

"He's beautiful," said Aunt Al, picking

the kitten up, while Tomboy wrapped herself around the old lady's thin bird's legs and made her steam-engine noise. "He's the spitting image of his mother. You'll miss him, won't you, Tomboy?"

"Nee-o."

"It's very nice of you to give him to me, Sophie," said Aunt Al. "Maybe I can give you something in return, one of these days."

Little did Sophie know, when she went to bed that night, what was covered over with an old sheet at the back of the garage.

Little did she guess, when she woke the next morning, what would be put in the potting-shed while she was at school, and while her great-great-aunt was paying a visit to the local pet-shop.

Little did she dream that, when she came

home that afternoon, Aunt Al would suggest a walk down to the potting-shed and then, before they went in, would say to her, "Shut your eyes, Sophie."

"Why?"

"Surprise."

Sophie shut her eyes and felt her hand held by another that was skinny and bony and curled like a bird's claws.

"OK," said Aunt Al. "You can look now."

There, sitting placidly in a large new rabbit-hutch, was a large new rabbit. A white rabbit with floppy ears and pink eyes and a wiffly nose.

"Yours," said Aunt Al.

"Yikes!" said Sophie.

Al beano, thought Sophie. Funny name.

SLOW AND STEADY
WINS THE RACE

Sophie hit upon a name for her rabbit quite simply.

"Why has he got pink eyes?" she asked Aunt Al.

"Because he's albino."

Al Beano, thought Sophie. Funny name, but if you take off the Al – after all, we've got one of those in the family – that just leaves Beano. I like that.

At first, Sophie was worried about Tomboy. What would she think of Beano? Cats killed little wild rabbits, she felt sure. What about big tame ones?

She found out the answer very soon after Beano's arrival, when he was hopping about the floor and Tomboy suddenly came in through the hole in the back of the shed. Sophie had looked round to see the black cat creeping forward, tail lashing. But before she could move, the big white rabbit first gave an almighty thump on the floor with his hind legs and then, with a kind of a growl, made a dash at Tomboy, who turned and fled.

Matthew and Mark did not share Sophie's feeling for animals. They were polite to Tomboy and to the new rabbit, but what they were mad about was sport. Their ambition was to play professional football (in the same team, of course, and in the First Division, naturally,) when they were grown-up.

The highlight of the summer term for them was the school sports day. Fast runners both, they were set on beating all

The big white rabbit gave an almighty thump on the floor.

the other boys of their age when the great day came.

Sophie was not a fast runner.

"But I would like to win something," she said to Beano as he lolloped around the floor of the potting-shed, while she cleaned out his hutch.

Sophie strewed fresh sawdust on the floor of the hutch, and filled the hayrack, the feeding dish and the water-bottle. "There you are, my dear," she said. "All nice and tidy. In you go, there's a good boy."

She used this last word with confidence. Admittedly, she'd been slightly wrong about Tom, and later about Molly, Holly and Polly, but Aunt Al had assured her that the pet-shop owner had assured *her* that the rabbit was definitely a buck.

She latched the door of the hutch and went to find her brothers.

They were practising baton-changing on the lawn, preparing for the lower junior boys' relay race.

"When it's sports day," she said to them, "what could I win?"

"How fast are you?" they said.

"Not very," said Sophie.

"Let's see," said Matthew.

"We'll give you a good start," said Mark.

"From the path here ..."

"... to the other end of the lawn."

"Ready?" said Matthew.

"Steady?" said Mark.

"Go!" they shouted.

Sophie plodded off at her best speed, shoulders hunched, arms pumping, a look of grim determination on her face, and when she was half-way across, the boys gave chase. They flashed past and stood waiting for her at the other end.

The twins seemed to go almost as fast
when bound together, as separately.

"You're not," said Mark.

"Not what?"

"Very fast," said Matthew.

They looked at one another thoughtfully.

"I know!" said Mark.

"I know what you're going to say!" said Matthew.

"The infants' three-legged race!" they cried.

"What's that?"

"Well, you have a partner ..."

"... and you stand next to him ..."

"... with your inside legs tied together ..."

"... so there's two legs on the outside and one in the middle."

"We'll show you," they said, and they ran off and came back with a piece of old rope.

Sophie watched them. They seemed to go almost as fast when bound together, as separately, so well balanced were they.

"You want to pick someone exactly your size," said Matthew.

"No good you partnering someone with great long legs," said Mark.

Sophie sat on a garden seat, rubbing the end of her nose.

"Exactly my size..." she said slowly.

So it was, that every playtime from then on Sophie and Andrew solemnly practised for the three-legged race.

At first they fell down a great deal, but then, because Sophie was determined they should succeed, they gradually improved, always remembering to start with the outside feet, and becoming used to a comfortable pattern of stride.

Matthew and Mark even took time off from their training to come and have a look at Sophie and Andrew in double harness.

"Not bad!" they said.

"Good balance."

"Nice rhythm."

"Steady pace."

"Take some beating!"

Sophie woke on the morning of sports day feeling quite confident that victory would be hers (and Andrew's of course). No other pair of infants could hold a candle to them, she was sure.

To cap it all, it was a lovely day, sunny and warm, and Sophie went happily to school. She did not worry that there was no sign of Andrew. He's late, she thought. But then the teacher called his name at registration and there was no answer!

The secretary put her head round the classroom door.

"Andrew's mother's just rung," she said.

"He's got the mumps."

"There's always the infants' egg-and-spoon race," the twins said when Sophie told them the terrible news at playtime.

"I'm not fast enough."

"You don't have to be fast for the egg-and-spoon," said Mark. "You just have to concentrate on the potato."

"What potato?"

"They don't actually use eggs," said Matthew. "And the fast ones always drop their potatoes."

"Just go steady," they said.

Nobody was surprised that afternoon when, between them, the twins won all the lower junior boys' races. Matthew just beat Mark in the sixty metres and Mark just beat Matthew in the hundred metres, and, thanks to the pair of them, their team easily won the relay.

Sophie had no such luck in the infants' races. She tried hard despite her disappointment over Andrew, but was usually among the last to finish. Worse however was to come.

"Now then," said the teacher who was organizing the three-legged race, "everybody stand beside their partners." And she went round tying legs together.

"Sophie," she said at last, "where's your partner?"

"He's got the mumps," said Sophie in a voice of deepest gloom.

"Then we must find you another. Now, who still hasn't got someone to run with?"

"Me, miss," said a voice. "Samantha's gone on holiday."

It was Dawn.

*When all the pairs were lined up, it was
plain that one was dreadfully unsuited.*

"Yuk!" said Sophie. "I don't want to run with her."

"Don't be silly, Sophie. Come here, Dawn."

When all the pairs were lined up for the race, it was only too plain that one was dreadfully unsuited. Lanky Dawn with her neat blonde ringlets towered over dark stocky Sophie, who looked, as always, as though she had just come through a hedge backwards. And it was very apparent that only the length of material binding them together stopped them from putting as much distance as possible between one another.

"Go!" shouted the teacher, and away went the other couples, their arms round each other's shoulders.

Now, all those minutes, hours even, of painstaking practice with poor, fat-necked

Andrew were as nothing. Sophie led off with her left foot and Dawn did the same, and they fell in a heap.

Struggling up, they stumbled and shambled behind – off balance, out of step, and hopelessly ill-matched. Time and again they fell, until at last Dawn burst into tears and lay, howling.

Sophie did not approve of crying. She was simply very angry.

"You wimp!" she said bitterly. "I ought to thump you. You're mowldy, stupid and assive, you are," and she undid the binding, got to her feet and stumped off.

"Hard luck, Sophie," said Matthew.

"It was that crummy Dawn," said Mark.

"There's still the egg-and-spoon race," said Matthew.

"Concentrate on the potato," said Mark.

*"You wimp!" Sophie said bitterly.
"I ought to thump you."*

"You can do it!" they said.

The potatoes were of all shapes and sizes, and by sheer good luck Sophie was given a nice heavy one that fitted well into the bowl of the spoon. That was a help, no doubt about it, but more important was the fact that Sophie remembered her brothers' advice to go steady.

Several of the infants galloped away at the start of the race, especially the still-snivelling Dawn who was anxious to get as far away from Sophie as she could. And before long potatoes were rolling everywhere on the grass.

Soon all the faster runners were in trouble. The race, it was plain, was between Sophie and Duncan – who was also going along very steadily, possibly because his short legs would carry him no faster.

Neck and neck they plodded on, while

the twins yelled encouragement to their sister, and then Duncan tripped and fell, and Sophie came home the winner.

That evening Sophie was sitting in the potting-shed, chatting to Beano as he polished off a carrot, when Tomboy appeared in the doorway. Having made sure that the rabbit was safely shut in his hutch, she came over to be stroked and petted.

"Shall I tell you something, Tomboy?" said Sophie. "Today I won the infants' egg-and-spoon race."

"Yee-oo?" said Tomboy.

"Yes, me. What do you think of that, my dear?" said Sophie.

Her black cat purred very loudly indeed.

*The twins were always rushing everywhere
and shouting at each other.*

LOST AND FOUND

Shortly after sports day, Matthew and Mark went to the seaside on a school camp. Sophie was too young to go. Not that she minded – she was fond of the twins, of course, but they were so noisy, always rushing everywhere and shouting at each other, that it would be nice to have a bit of peace and quiet for one week out of the fifty-two. Besides she had Tomboy and Beano for company.

"Poor Sophie, she'll be lonely," said her mother.

"She'll miss the boys, I expect," said her father.

"Perhaps," said her mother, "we ought to give her a special treat, to make up for not being able to go to camp?"

"Good idea," said her father, "but what?" They thought for a minute.

"I know!" said Sophie's father.

"I know what you're going to say!" said Sophie's mother, and then they grinned at one another.

"We sound just like the twins!" they said.

Hanging on Sophie's bedroom walls were four pictures, all drawn by Sophie's mother. One was of a cow called Blossom, one was of two hens named April and May, the third was of a Shetland pony called Shorty and the fourth was of a spotty pig by the name of Measles. These were the animals that would one day belong to Sophie when she was a grown-up lady farmer.

That evening, when her parents came in to say goodnight to her, Sophie was sitting up in bed, underneath her portrait gallery, looking at a picture book. It was, of course, about a farm. On its cover was a picture of a rather fat farmer and a surprised-looking cow. Instead of sitting on a stool and milking the cow into a pail, the farmer was sitting on the pail and milking her into the upturned stool.

"Look what he's doing!" Sophie's father said, pointing.

"He's forgettable," said Sophie.

"Don't you mean 'forgetful'?" said her mother.

"I've forgotten," said Sophie.

"Well, just remember," her father said, "when you're grown-up and milking your cows, not to be as absent-minded as that."

"I shall have a milking-machine," said Sophie.

"What, for just one cow?"

"I shall have lots of cows. Blossom will have lots of calves, and then they'll grow up and have calves of their own, and soon I'll have hundreds."

"How would you like to see hundreds of cows?" her mother said.

"All different breeds," said her father.

"And masses of pigs."

"And loads of sheep."

"And horses and ponies."

"And hens and ducks and geese."

"And rabbits?" said Sophie.

"Yes, probably."

"And cats?"

"No. No cats. But every kind of farm animal you can think of, as well as tractors and all sorts of machines. At the Royal

Wessex Agricultural Show. Tomorrow. Would you like to go?"

"Yikes!" shouted Sophie. "I shan't sleep a wink!"

"Oh, yes you will," they said. "You have a good night's rest. Sleep tight and mind the fleas don't bite."

They tucked her in, kissed her goodnight and turned off the light. Sophie lay wide awake for what seemed to her like ages. I shall never get to sleep, she said to herself after about ten minutes – I'm so excited about tomorrow.

She began to count sheep jumping through a hole in a hedge. At the fifteenth sheep she gave a tremendous yawn and at the twenty-seventh her eyes closed. Next thing she knew, it was broad daylight.

Sophie sat up and looked at her bedside clock. The little hand pointed to six, the big

"Wakey, wakey! Rise and shine!" said Sophie.

hand to eight.

"Half-past eight!" she cried. "Mummy and Dad must have overslept. We'll all be late getting to the Agricultural Show!"

She leapt out of bed and ran to her parents' bedroom. Yes, there they were – fast asleep still!

"Wakey, wakey! Rise and shine!" said Sophie.

They raised bleary faces, and Sophie's father peered at his watch.

"What sort of time d'you call this?" he mumbled.

"Half-past eight."

Sophie's father sighed.

"It's the little hand that points to the hour," he said, "and the big hand to the minutes. It's twenty to six."

About five hours later (it seemed to Sophie

like five years), they arrived at the Royal Wessex Agricultural Society's showground. Never in her life had Sophie seen so many people – people of all ages, from very old ones being pushed about in wheelchairs to very young ones being pushed about in prams.

"We shall never see any of the animals with all that crowd," she said.

"Oh yes, we will," her mother said. "But don't go wandering off, Sophie. You stay by us."

"We don't want you getting lost," her father said. "Now then, where shall we start? Cattle? Pigs? Sheep?"

"Hot dogs," said Sophie.

"But you've just had breakfast."

"I'm starving."

"It's a very warm day for eating hot dogs."

"Where shall we start?" asked Sophie's father.
"Hot dogs," said Sophie.

"Not if you have an ice-cream after," said Sophie.

In the dairy cattle lines they found Friesians and Ayrshires and Shorthorns and Guernseys and beautiful little doe-eyed Jersey cows, one of which, Sophie said, was exactly what Blossom would be like, one day.

Amongst all the hens in the poultry tent there were two sitting side by side – the spitting images of April and May. And as they walked towards the pig lines, along came a girl leading a Shetland pony that was Shorty to the life. All I've got to do now, thought Sophie, is to see a pig just like Measles. But there was such a press of people in the pig lines, almost all of them much taller and wider than Sophie, that she had a job to spot a single pig, let alone a spotty one.

After a bit, she caught a glimpse of some pinky-white ones, and some black ones, and even some ginger ones with very long snouts, but nothing that looked remotely like Measles.

Sophie, though small, was very determined, and she was not going to give up easily. One minute she was walking along behind her mother and father, and the next, catching sight of a white pig with a dark spot on it, she turned and began to burrow her way through the crowd to get closer to its pen.

But when at last she reached it, she was disappointed to see that it only had two or three spots. She wriggled her way along to the next pen, and the next, but the pigs in these again only had a few spots.

The fourth pen was different. Not that the animal in it was any spottier, but there was a notice above it, which Sophie could not read, and in the pen, brushing the pig's bristly back, was a man.

Sophie decided to consult him. She knew that children should not speak to strange men, but she badly needed this one's help, and anyway he looked a nice, kind man. He was fat, with a pink face and a squashy nose and rather big ears. In fact he looked a good deal like the pig that he was grooming.

"Excuse me," Sophie said. "Could you tell me what this notice says?"

The pigman stopped his brushing and looked up.

"It do say 'Gloucester Old Spots', young lady," he replied. "That's the name of the breed, see?"

"Oh," said Sophie. "They don't have many spots, do they?"

"Not nowadays," said the pigman. "'Tidn't the fashion no more. Time was, thisyer breed was covered in spots."

"Like someone with measles?" Sophie said.

The pigman made a deep grunting noise which, since he was smiling, Sophie took to be a laugh.

"You interested in pigs then, are you, young lady?" he said.

"Yes," said Sophie. "I'm going to be a lady farmer when I grow up."

"Oh ar. And you fancies a pig with a girt lot of spots on, do you?"

"Yes."

"Well, you might be lucky. Some piglets is born with plenty, now and again."

"Thanks," said Sophie. "Goodbye."

"Cheerio," said the pigman.

He looked over Sophie's head and said,

"Well I never!" said the pigman. "Lost your mum and dad in the crowd, have you, young lady?"

"I reckon she'll make a proper farmer, your little girl will."

Sophie turned round to see a perfectly strange man and woman standing behind her.

"The child is nothing to do with us," the man said.

"Disgraceful," the woman said, "the way some people let little children wander about on their own," and they walked away.

"Well I never!" said the pigman. "Lost your mum and dad in the crowd, have you, young lady?"

Sophie nodded. How shall I ever find them again? she thought. Many children would have cried, but Sophie did not approve of crying.

"Don't you fret," said the pigman. "I'll tell you what to do. See that tent over there with a flag flying over it?"

Sophie nodded again.

"That's the Secretary's tent, that is. You go straight there and tell 'em your name, and they'll put it out on the Tannoy. I'd come with you myself but I can't leave thisyer sow, we'm due in the show-ring in a couple of minutes."

Sophie plodded off towards the Secretary's tent, and when she was half-way there she heard the blare of a loudspeaker.

"Here is an announcement," said a voice. "Will a little girl called Sophie come to the Secretary's tent, where her parents are waiting for her?"

"Well, I'm coming, aren't I?" said Sophie crossly, and then she saw her mother and father standing outside the tent, looking anxiously around. When they caught sight of her, they ran to meet her.

"Oh darling!" her mother cried as she

grabbed Sophie and hugged her. "We've been worried stiff!"

"Where on earth did you get to?" her father said.

"I was just having a conservation," Sophie said.

"A conservation?"

"With a nice pigman."

"Don't you mean a 'conversation'?"

"That's what I said. We were talking."

"What about?"

"Pigs, of course. Can I have another hot dog?"

"Oh, Sophie!" they said.

"And another ice-cream."

Sophie was walking Beano
round the lawn on a lead.

"MUCH TOO YOUNG"

Sophie was walking Beano round the lawn on a lead.

At one time, before the arrival of the rabbit, she had had the idea of treating Tomboy in a similar fashion. After all, people took their dogs for walks – why not their cats? So she had opened her piggy-bank and used some of the precious Farm Munny to buy a little collar and lead.

Tomboy had submitted to the fitting of the collar, but when Sophie attached the lead to it and said, "Come on, Tomboy! Walkies!" the black cat had simply lain on her back and batted at the lead with her forepaws like a kitten playing with a piece of string. Tugging, Sophie found, only produced growls and tail-lashings, so she gave up the attempt at cat-walking. She had left the collar on because she thought it looked nice – it was a blue one – until Aunt Al had told her that it was dangerous for an outdoor cat to wear a collar.

"It might get caught on a twig when Tomboy was tree-climbing, you see," she had said, "and then she'd choke herself."

So Sophie had hung up collar and lead in the potting-shed until such time as she should be allowed a puppy of her own, something which she was hopeful would happen one day.

In the mean time, Beano had arrived, and one morning Sophie tried the blue collar on him. It fitted perfectly – it looked rather nice against his snowy fur and he did not seem to object. "And," said Sophie, "one thing's certain – you won't be climbing any trees." So she left it round his neck.

Beano's hutch was positioned low down, merely raised above the floor of the shed by the height of the four bricks it stood on. This had been done partly because Sophie was not tall, but chiefly so that the rabbit could hop out and down when Sophie was cleaning the hutch, and then hop up and back in again easily. The potting-shed door was of course kept shut at these times. Watching him lolloping about on the floor in his new blue collar, Sophie suddenly thought how much he might enjoy a walk on grass.

She clipped the lead on to the collar and opened the door of the shed. For a few moments Beano sat in the doorway, wiffling his nose madly at all the scents of the garden, and then he hopped out, Sophie following.

She soon found that though you may take a dog for a walk, going wherever you wish, that's not the case with a rabbit. The rabbit takes you for the walk and goes wherever it pleases.

But there was no doubt that Beano was greatly enjoying this new experience. He

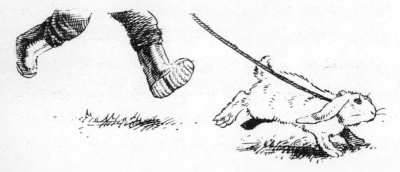

hopped about all over the lawn, sometimes so quickly that Sophie had to run to keep up, and now and again he gave a little buck-jump of excitement. At first he pleased himself entirely where he went – into the flowerbeds and then into the vegetable patch – until Sophie hit upon a way, if not to lead him, at least to steer him roughly in the direction she wanted. On their next outing she held the lead in one hand and in the other a Special Rabbit Controller which she had invented. This was a flat square of stout cardboard which she had fixed on to the end of a bamboo cane, and by holding it, for example, on the left side of Beano's face, she forced him to turn right. She had got the idea from remembering how the pigmen at the Royal Wessex Agricultural Show had driven their charges to and from the show-ring by using screens to direct them. (Her nice pigman had, to her delight, won the breed championship with his Gloucester Old Spots sow.) Now, using the Special Rabbit Controller, she could steer the rabbit away from her mother's dahlias or her father's cabbages, and could guide him back into the potting-shed at the end of the outing.

Each day (for by now the summer holidays had arrived) Beano took Sophie for a walk on the grass.

One morning Sophie's father sat on the swing-seat by the edge of the lawn reading the Sunday papers and watching Sophie controlling her rabbit (with difficulty, for Beano was in a contrary mood).

"What you need, Sophie," he said, "is a Labour-saving Device."

"What's that mean?"

"I'll show you," her father said. "I've had an idea that will take all the hard work out of rabbit-exercising."

He got up and went to his workshop at the back of the garage, and came back in a little while with a hammer and a long iron spike which he drove into the lawn.

"Now then," he said, "drop the loop on the end of the lead over the spike, and then Beano can go round and round, so far and no further, and get his exercise and his grazing, and you can put your feet up."

"Daddy," said Sophie, "you're brill."

She sat beside him on the swing-seat and

watched Beano, now safely tethered, nibbling happily away in the sunshine, and presently Tomboy came stalking across the lawn, keeping carefully out of the range of the rabbit, and jumped up on her lap, purring fit to bust.

My own black cat and my own white rabbit, thought Sophie. Who could ask for anything more?

"Daddy?" she said. "When can I have a puppy?"

"Not till you're old enough."

"I'm six this Christmas." (Sophie's birthday was on Christmas Day.)

"Much too young."

"Seven?"

"No."

"Eight then?"

"Possibly."

"Daddy, when can I have a puppy?"

Sophie rubbed the tip of her nose.

"Matthew and Mark are eight," she said.

"So?"

"So they're old enough to have a puppy. Only of course they'll need two – one each."

Her father laid down his newspaper.

"I can read you like a book, madam," he said. "You know the twins aren't all that interested in animals, so if they were allowed a puppy (and you can forget about two, right now), you'd take it over. That was what you were thinking, wasn't it?"

Sophie did not approve of telling lies so she said, "Yes."

"You've got your own black cat and your own rabbit."

"Yes."

"Well then."

Sophie sat silent on the swing-seat for

some little time, while her father rocked it gently with one foot as he read his paper, and Tomboy purred, and Beano grazed.

Then she said, "Andrew's only five like me and he's got three dogs."

"Andrew?"

"Yes. You know. Where I fell in the cowpat."

"Oh, the farmer's son."

"Yes. He's got three."

"Fancy."

"Two sheepdogs and a terrier called Lucy."

"But they aren't his dogs, are they? They're his father's dogs."

"Yes. But he's lucky, Andrew is, all the same."

There was another silence, broken only by the purr of the cat and a little squeaking noise as the seat swung to and fro.

"Isn't he?" said Sophie.

"Isn't who what?"

"Andrew. Lucky."

"Mm."

Silence again for a moment. Tomboy jumped down and walked away. Beano sat up and scratched his ear. The seat squeaked.

"She's going to have babies, sometime later on this year, Andrew told me," said Sophie.

"Who is?"

"Lucy."

Sophie's father sighed and folded his newspaper.

"Sophie love," he said, "I've read the same sentence about five times. How about going and asking Mum if she'd put the kettle on? I wouldn't mind a mug of coffee."

And I wouldn't mind one of Lucy's puppies when she has them, thought Sophie as she plodded off. It's not fair. Fancy having to wait till I'm eight. That's nearly two and a half years. And then they'll probably still say "No". I wish I was grown up.

"Mum," she said, when she had given the message. "When you were a child, did you have a dog of your very own?"

"Yes, I did, Sophie. When Granpa and Granny thought I was responsible enough to look after it properly – to feed it and groom it and train it and exercise it. 'You shall have a puppy of your own,' they said, 'once you're old enough.'"

"And how old was that?"

"Twelve."

That evening, when the children were all in bed, Sophie's father said to his wife, "Did

*"When I was a boy, I always
wanted a little terrier."*

you have a dog of your own when you were a child?"

"How odd!" she replied. "Sophie asked me that, this morning."

"Really?"

"Yes, and I told her I did, but not till I was twelve. They didn't think I was old enough till then."

"Ah. What sort was it?"

"A little terrier."

"Funny," said Sophie's father. "I wasn't allowed a dog of my own when I was a boy, but I always wanted a little terrier."

"Do you still?"

Sophie's father laughed. "I'm certainly old enough now," he said.

Sophie's mother laughed. "Me too," she said.

*One day the twins came home in
a state of high excitement.*

ONE FINAL PRESENT

Before you could look round, it seemed to Sophie, those sunny summer holidays were over and the children were going back to school.

Matthew and Mark had nearly always gone off to play football with their friends, so Sophie had really only seen them at mealtimes.

It was much the same at school, except that now it was proper football with a proper pitch and goalposts.

One day the twins came home in a state of high excitement.

"What's up with you two?" their mother said. "Scored a goal each, have you?"

"No, Mum," said Mark. "It's the school concert."

"You know," said Matthew. "At the end of this term."

"We've got parts in the juniors' play!" they said.

"I wish I could be in a play," said Sophie.

"You might be," said Matthew.

"The infants do one too, you know," said Mark.

"Who d'you think we're going to be, Mum?" said Matthew.

"Have a guess," said Mark.

"I don't even know what the play is," said their mother. "You'll have to tell me that first."

"It's all different bits out of *Alice in Wonderland*," said Mark.

"And *Alice through the Looking-Glass*," said Matthew.

"All put together," they said.

"You're a crazy couple," said their mother. "I should think you're going to be the Mad Hatter and the March Hare."

"No!" they shouted.

"I'm Tweedledum!" said Matthew.

"And I'm Tweedledee!" said Mark.

"And we're going to be all stuffed out with cushions …"

"… to make us look fat …"

"… and have a great battle …"

"… with toy swords!"

"Football and fighting!" said Sophie scornfully when the twins had run whooping away. "That's all boys think about."

"Perhaps you'll get a nice part in the infants' play," her mother said.

The very next day, as it happened, Sophie's

*"Whose birthday do we celebrate
on Christmas Day?" asked the teacher.
"Mine," said Sophie.*

teacher said to her class, "Now, after the end of this term, there's a very special day to look forward to. Who can tell me what it is called?"

A forest of hands shot up.

"Well, Dawn?"

"It's Christmas Day."

"And what's special about Christmas Day? Andrew?"

"You get lots of presents."

"That's not what I meant. Yes, Duncan?"

"You get a lot to eat."

"No, no," said the teacher. "Never mind about presents or food. Christmas Day is special because that's when we celebrate a very important birthday. And whose birthday is that?"

"Mine," said Sophie.

The teacher looked hard at Sophie. Then she opened her register and ran a finger down the class list of dates of birth.

Then she said, "Yes, Sophie, I remember now that your birthday is on Christmas Day. But I'm talking about a baby who was born nearly two thousand years ago, in Bethlehem."

Dawn's long skinny arm was raised.

"Yes, Dawn?"

"Jesus."

"Yes, that's right, good girl. Now you all remember the story of Jesus's birth, don't you? He was born in a stable, wasn't He?"

"Yes."

"Why?"

"They were full up in the pub," said Sophie.

"I don't think that's the right word to use, Sophie," said the teacher. "It was simply an inn where travellers rested. But yes, there was no room at the inn, so the baby was born in the stable and laid in a manger. What's a manger, someone? Andrew?"

"It's like a wooden trough," said Andrew. "You put hay in it. But we don't."

"Why not?"

"We make silage."

"Oh. I see. Anyway, this is what I want to tell you all. At the end of this term we shall have the school concert, and this class is going to act its own little play, all about the birth of Jesus. There'll be Mary and Joseph and the Wise Men and the shepherds and the innkeeper and … now who have I forgotten?"

"The ox and the ass," said Sophie. "That could be me and Andrew, couldn't it?"

"No, Sophie, the animals will just be painted on the scenery. Now who will be the most important person in the whole play?"

"Baby Jesus!" they all chorused.

"Please, miss," said Duncan. "Can I be Baby Jesus?"

"He's small enough," said Sophie drily.

"No, no, Duncan, the baby will be represented by a doll. I couldn't have a live baby on the stage."

"You wouldn't have time," said Sophie.

"It takes nine months, like a cow," said Andrew.

Possibly these last two remarks had something to do with the fact that, when the leading parts in the play were allotted, Sophie and Andrew were passed over.

"Don't worry," said the teacher to those without starring roles. "You'll all be dressing up and singing 'Once in Royal David's City'."

"I'm in the infants' play," said Sophie that evening.

"Oh good," said her father. "Who else in your class is in it?"

"Everyone."

"Oh. What's it about?"

"It's an activity play."

"Don't you mean a 'nativity' play?"

"No, it's about Baby Jesus being born."

"Are you Mary?" said Mark.

"No."

"Who is?" said Matthew.

"Dawn," said Sophie.

"Yuk!" they said.

"Well, you can't be Joseph …"

"… or a Wise Man …"

"… or a shepherd …"

"… or the innkeeper …"

"… because they'll all be boys …"

"… so who are you?"

"I'm a crowd," said Sophie.

"Well, at least you won't have any words

"That's no good," said Sophie. *"It's a girl."*

to learn then," her mother said.

"Except rhubarb, rhubarb, rhubarb," said her father.

"Why rhubarb?"

"That's what everyone says in crowd scenes."

Later, when the infant class had the first rehearsal of their Christmas play, Sophie and Andrew and the rest of the extras stood at the back of the stage, while Joseph and Mary and the innkeeper and the Wise Men and the shepherds were pushed and pulled into their proper places.

Mary, Dawn that is, had brought in to school a bald baby doll of her own, and had beforehand been preparing to wrap its bare pink body in swaddling clothes, when Sophie had chanced by.

"That's no good," she said.

"Why not?" said Dawn.

"You blind?" said Sophie. "It's a girl."

But now Mary sat nursing the baby, Joseph standing proudly at her side, and on came the shepherds and the Wise Men bearing their gifts which they presented. But all the time no one said anything, not a word.

Sophie looked about at all the others in the crowd, but they too were silent. Sillies,

she thought, they don't know what to say.
But I do, and loudly she cried, "Rhubarb,
rhubarb, rhubarb!"

"Anybody would think rhubarb was a rude
word," said Sophie afterwards to an
audience of two, Tomboy and Beano.

"Nee-o," said Tomboy.

"Well, the teacher got ever so mad with
me, and I was only doing what Dad said.

She's mowldy, stupid and assive, that's what she is."

Not long after the half-term break, Andrew said to Sophie, "Lucy's got puppies."

"How many?" said Sophie.

"Six."

"Yikes!"

"You can come and see them if you like."

Sophie hesitated. She longed to see the puppies, but she knew it would be awful because she would want one of them so much.

Unwittingly, Andrew made matters worse.

"You could have one when they're old enough," he said.

"No," said Sophie. "They won't let me. Not till I'm eight."

"Well, d'you want to see them or not?

Make your mind up."

Sophie made it up.

"OK," she said. "I'd better come to tea. You ask your mummy to ask my mummy if I can."

Sophie never forgot the first time she set eyes on that litter of six fat little terrier puppies. They were a fortnight old, their eyes not long opened, and they were just beginning to stumble about on their short legs.

All puppies are delightful creatures, especially to someone who is determined to become a lady farmer.

Lucy, the mother, was a smooth-haired small white terrier with some black patches.

"But the father of the pups," said Andrew's father, "was brown and white, so most of these have got some brown on

"Which one do you like best, Sophie?"
asked Andrew's father.

them too. Which one do you like best, Sophie?"

Sophie rubbed the tip of her nose.

"That one," she said, and she pointed to a puppy that was all white except for a black patch over his right eye. "I just wish I could have him."

"Well, I'm going to sell the lot when they're old enough," said the farmer. "You'd better ask your mum and dad."

"They won't let me," said Sophie. "They say I'm too young."

"And how old are you?"

"I'll be six on Christmas Day."

"Will you indeed?" said Andrew's father. "Well, they're right. You are too young to have a dog of your own, same as Andrew here. Haven't your family a dog at all?"

"No."

"No animals?"

"I've got a cat and a rabbit," Sophie said.

"Ah well, you aren't doing too badly then. I dare say they'll get a dog one day. Come on then, Lucy – in you go with your pups. And Andrew and Sophie – it's time for tea."

With one last backward look at the white puppy with the black patch over his right eye, Sophie plodded off. I don't want to see them again, she said to herself. If Andrew asks me to tea before they're all sold, I shan't go. I couldn't bear it.

In fact, Andrew did not ask her again as November and the early part of December sped by, and soon the school concert was upon them.

Sophie's mother and father came with all the other parents to watch.

The nativity play went pretty well except that one of the Wise Men was silly enough to drop his gift. Sophie, wrapped in a red-checked gingham tablecloth and positioned at the rear of the crowd, remained silent, only mouthing "Rhubarb" when she caught her parents' eyes.

As for Tweedledum, he had the most tremendous fight with Tweedledee for stealing his nice new rattle, and, all in all, the concert was a great success.

Hardly was it over, it seemed to Sophie, than it was Christmas Eve, the eve of her sixth birthday.

Christmas Day began as usual – the stockings, then breakfast, then the giving out of the presents, all stacked beneath the Christmas tree. Just before they started on that, the phone rang and it was Aunt Al, to wish them the compliments of the season.

When it was Sophie's turn to speak, she said, "How's Ollie?"

"He's fine," said Aunt Al. "He's grown. He's going to be the biggest cat in the Highlands, I should think."

"As big as a Scottish Wild Cat?"

"Shouldn't wonder. Have you had any good presents?"

"We haven't opened them yet."

"Hope you get a nice surprise," said Aunt Al.

As always, the presents were opened one at a time, youngest first. One for Sophie, then one for Mark, then Matthew, then Mummy, then Dad, and finally a birthday present for Sophie before she began again on her next Christmas one.

But this year, when all the presents had been undone and there was nothing left under the tree, Sophie's father said, "Now everybody stay put and play with your presents. I shan't be more than quarter of an hour," and out he went.

They heard the car start up.

"Where's Dad gone, Mum?" said Matthew.

"To fetch something."

"What is it?" said Mark.

"One final present."

"Who's it for?" said Sophie.

"All of us."

"For all of us?" said the three children with one voice.

"Yes. It's for Daddy and it's for me and it's for Matthew and it's for Mark and it's for Sophie."

The twins shook their heads.

"I don't get it," said Mark.

"Me neither," said Matthew.

As for Sophie, she suddenly remembered that in all the excitement she had fed

The door opened, and in walked their father,
carrying something in his arms.

neither Tomboy nor Beano, and she went off to give each a special Christmas breakfast.

No sooner was she back in the sitting-room with the others than they all heard the car returning.

"Sit still," their mother said. "Don't move."

The door opened, and in walked their father, carrying something in his arms.

When Sophie saw what it was, for once in her life she did not shout "Yikes!" because her throat had suddenly tightened up so that she could not have got the sound out. And for once, though she did not approve of crying, her eyes filled with tears. They were tears of happiness, at the sight of the puppy that was all white except for a black patch over his right eye.

THE

END